Dying to Dance (Cha, Cha, Ahhh)
(A Tucson Valley Retirement Community Cozy Mystery Series)
By: Marcy Blesy

This book is a work of fiction. Names, characters, places, and events are a result of the imagination of the author or are used fictitiously. Any resemblance to actual persons, living or dead, businesses, events, or locations is a coincidence.

No part of the text may be reproduced without the written permission of the author, except for brief passages in reviews.

Copyright © 2024 by Marcy Blesy, LLC. All rights reserved. Cover design by Cormar Covers

Chapter 1

It's my turn to sit in the airport arrival's lane in Tucson as I await my parents' return to the Tucson Valley Retirement Community. They've been gone for nearly seven months, and I've missed them more than I could imagine. I look out my car window, watching the other snowbirds who are arriving in Arizona in November. Many won't come until after Christmas, but some, like my parents, have decided to give up any time in the Midwest when there is a chance of snow, and that pretty much falls between November and April in Illinois.

I see the wildly waving hands of my mother before I see her face. She wears a light tan jacket with blue jeans and a gray and white cardigan sweater. Dressing for a plane ride from the cold temperatures up north to the delightfully warm temperatures in Arizona in November is always a challenge. She pulls a suitcase behind her while Dad, lagging behind, pulls two additional suitcases. They'd decided to keep a car in storage in Tucson Valley rather than drive back and forth. I think it was a smart decision. That's a very long drive across the country. I study Dad before getting out of the car. He wears a navy blue polo shirt and khakis, his go-to golf attire. I've never seen him walk with more pep in his step, his knee surgery in February being a huge success. I open my car door and walk to the sidewalk on the other side of the car.

"Rosi!" Mom lets go of her suitcase and throws her arms around my body smashing me against her chest. "It's so good to see you again. You have been through some *things*."

I know she is referencing the bathtub *incident* in Phoenix and the construction site *distraction,* but I'd be fine if I never spoke of those things again. "Hi, Mom. It's really good to see you too."

When she lets go, Dad is standing with outstretched arms. At 40, it's a bit odd to be embraced as if I am a child, but I am not complaining. Somehow, my moving to Tucson Valley has brought us closer even though we lived in Springfield mere miles from each other for most of my adult life.

Dad puts his hands on my shoulders as he assesses me. There is nothing sweeter in this world than the smile of my dad. "You look radiant, Rosisophia Doroche."

Radiant may have been an overstatement, but it feels good to have some color in my otherwise pasty skin this time of year. And I've been using the exercise bikes in the technology center. I've biked in the Tour de France and the Black Hills of South Dakota—all virtually, but either way I'm toning up muscles that haven't been touched in years. "Thanks, Dad. Let me help you both with your bags."

The first stop on our way into Tucson Valley is the Doggie Care Center that Barley has been attending when I'm too busy at work to keep tabs on her. Tracy had wanted to keep her since it's a workday, but I reminded her that Gabby was coming by to help Mario replace the floor on the stage and that the noise of the saws and nail guns might drive Barley batty, and that would drive *her* batty too. With the Southwest Arizona Senior Dancing with the Pros Competition coming to the performing arts center next week—well, at least the tryouts—we thought it was time to upgrade the floor or we'd risk higher insurance premiums with dancers tripping and falling over loose floorboards.

"Mom, you might want to trade places with Dad, or Barley's going to get dog hair all over your sweater," I say, as I glance at my mom in the rearview mirror.

"It's fine, Rosi. I've kind of missed that silly pup."

"She still behaves like a pup, but she's grown a lot. I'm only preparing you!"

"I'm fine."

"Suit yourself." When I walk into the Doggie Care Center, I'm met by a chorus of barking that ranges from deep growls to high-pitch yapping.

"Rosi! Thank goodness you are here!" says Stacy, one of the owners. Her ponytail hangs loose on her neck with strands of hair sticking out in every direction. She looks like she's been on the losing end of a fight.

"Is everything okay?" I ask, concerned for the young woman.

"Barley!" She blows a strand of hair out of her mouth. "Barley has a lot of energy today, like more than usual. And diarrhea too. She's been going in and out like crazy. But it's her running around and around that's getting the other dogs all riled up that's been a bit much."

I look past Stacy into the common area. All the dogs, from the small dachshunds to the large mastiff and everything in between, are chasing a single dog around the room. The dog is Barley. She looks as if she's possessed, racing circles around the dogs she is simultaneously chasing. "I am so sorry! I have no idea what got into her."

"Could she have eaten something? Did you give her something you shouldn't have?"

I don't appreciate the judgment, so I clench and unclench my fists a few times before answering. "No, Stacy. I did not give my dog anything that I should not have given her."

"Whatever the cause, I think she should stay home for a few days. Until she can…uh…behave."

"My dog is being expelled?" I can feel my face getting warm.

"Not expelled. That's permanent. Think of it more like a suspension." She smiles weakly, as if that makes the situation better. Stacy doesn't wait for my response. She grabs Barley's leash off the wall and opens the gate into the common area. All the dogs but Barley run to her, seeing her as a savior of sorts from my hyperactive dog. "Barley, come," she commands. The fact that Stacy is the assistant teacher in Barley's puppy obedience class doesn't help with my feeling of incompetence as a dog mama when Barley positions herself in the farthest corner of the room, ready for a battle of wills.

"This is ridiculous. My parents are waiting in the car." I open the gate.

"Rosi! No!"

I hear Stacy's words, but I don't fully comprehend their meaning until I am being knocked over by the tail of the large mastiff as ten or twelve pairs of paws walk over my stomach, running into the waiting room and down the hallway to the staff offices. Only a cocker spaniel, Barley's friend Grayson, stays long enough to lick the wrinkles from the frown on my face.

"There's a double lock on the gate. You didn't lock the second lock." More strands of hair fall on Stacy's face, plastered by the sweat from her brow as she chases after the dogs trying to herd them. Dewey, the other owner of Doggie Care Center and Barley's lead teacher, has exited his office to help Stacy.

I get up from the ground, picking dog hair from my black capris. When I look up, Barley stands on the other side of the gate, sitting like an innocent girl, her tongue hanging from the side of her mouth. "You're a good girl, Barley. I don't care what that meanie says."

I leave thirty-five dollars on the counter, pick up Barley's leash from the ground where Stacy had dropped it, open the gate, leash up my obedient*ish* dog, and return to my parents. Mom is more than willing to be accosted by her sixty-pound granddog in the back seat of my car.

Chapter 2

"What did the vet say?" asks Keaton. He dries his hair from his shower which he's taken at my house after his gym workout.

"He said she will be fine once things run through her system. Thankfully, she ate the gallon of *vanilla* ice cream and not the pint of dark chocolate that was next to it in the open freezer. That could have been much more disastrous."

"Did he have any suggestions as to how she was able to use her paws to open the freezer?"

"We will never know. My dog is a Houdini."

"She keeps you on your toes. Will you ever take her back to classes or daycare again?" His grin could not get much wider.

"You think this is funny, don't you?" I ask, playfully.

"Well, since we know Barley is going to be okay, I feel like I have permission to at least guffaw silently. You described the scene so well." He laughs as he pats Barley on the head—the same Barley that hasn't moved from my yellow recliner since we returned home.

"The poor thing wiped herself out," I say, sinking onto the couch across from her.

"When are we supposed to meet your parents for dinner?" Keaton asks as he joins me on the couch.

"5:00. At Casa de Comidas."

"Ahh, do you think you can handle it?"

"What do you mean?" I ask, turning to look at him.

"Well, the last time you ate there, you had to leave to get sick—when we met Oliver?"

"That wasn't the worst thing that happened that night," I say quietly, recalling my walk through the construction site of what is now the amazing Roland Price Technology Center.

"True, but let's think happy thoughts." He looks at his watch, a goofy grin spreading across his face.

"What's that look for?"

"I was thinking we might have a little time to kill before we leave."

"Time for what?" I ask, playing along.

"I don't know, maybe something that would require a change."

"What kind of change?'

"A change of clothes. I most definitely think you need to change your clothes. Black is not your color."

"I suppose you know what I should wear?" I tease.

"Not in the least. Let's go to your closet, and you can try a few things on." He winks, and my heart flutters.

We are ten minutes late when we walk into Casa de Comidas. It takes everything I have to subdue my laughter when Mom asks if we got stuck in traffic because there is never traffic in Tucson Valley.

Keaton covers nicely though. "Renee! Richard! It's so nice to see you both again. We stopped at my place to get this," he says, pulling out a succulent plant from a bag he was carrying, something I hadn't even noticed.

"Keaton! You are always so thoughtful. Thank you. I love it." After embracing both of us, she returns to her seat next to my dad who reaches his hand across the table to shake Keaton's hand.

"Hi, everyone," I say too enthusiastically as I wave at the rest of the people seated around the table.

Karen sits next to Bob, his hand over the top of hers. She has the sweetest demeanor that she shares with everyone she meets, whether she likes them or not. You never know Karen's true thoughts about a person because, though quiet, she emanates a gentle, kind mood all the time. They wear matching green sweaters that say *Arizona Retiree* that I imagine Karen embroidered. Next to Bob is Frank who has a large beer in front of him. Jan, his wife, meets my eyes with a scowl on her face. Ever since I rebuffed her nephew Allen, she's been sour on me though I thought for a moment we had a breakthrough at the Senior Living Retirement Community Conference in Phoenix when she'd shared a sweet story about her mother. But as soon as we returned to Tucson Valley, she and Brenda slipped back into their roles as the community crabbies. I don't much care anymore though. I have better things to do with my time than to worry about whether Jan Jinkins or Brenda Riker likes me.

Speaking of Brenda, she sits next to Jan. Unlike Jan who is wearing a denim vest over a shirt with a large cactus, Brenda wears a tight-fitting black shirt with deep enough cleavage to make a target for a mini basketball. A man that I do not know sits next to her. He's quite tall as his head nearly grazes the pendant light that hangs closest to his head. His well-trimmed, peppered mustache matches his full head of hair, and he has the most beautiful, sincere smile. What a striking gentleman.

Brenda answers my unasked question when she announces to Keaton and me, "This is Amos Aleger. He is my new friend." I've never seen Brenda smile for so long. I didn't know that the muscles along her mouth could hold in place to produce such a beautiful smile.

"Nice to meet you, Amos," says Keaton, holding out his hand to the charming man who takes my hand first—which I'd also extended—and places a kiss atop it.

Paula sits at the head of the table. "Nice to see ya again, Rosi. That technology center sure is a beauty." She adjusts her hearing aid as she awaits my reply.

"Yes, thanks, Paula. We are really proud of what's happening in Tucson Valley. Make sure you take a virtual reality vacation. They are fantastic." Keaton pulls out my chair next to Mom, and I sit down. Dad pushes the chip bowl in my direction.

"And don't forget the digital art wall. That was *my* idea, you know?" Amos can't stop staring at Brenda as she gloats, much as Salem Mansfield once held a certain spell over the men in the retirement community.

13

"I can't wait to check out all of these new things," Mom says, clapping her hands. "I am so excited."

"Yes, we are happy to be back in Tucson Valley with our friends. Thank you all for agreeing to meet with us tonight," says Dad as he holds up his beer bottle. "To another great winter in the world of retirement!"

Everyone holds up their drinks, Keaton and I glasses of water since we haven't ordered yet. "Cheers!"

There are so many conversations happening at the same time that I don't focus on any one topic, instead letting myself relax as I sip my margarita which has arrived just in time to counter the ill effects of spicy salsa that hits me in the back of my throat.

"So, when Allen wins the Southwest Arizona Senior Dancing with the Pros Competition, he's going to use the prize money to take his lovely girlfriend to Hawaii. Doesn't that sound wonderful?" Jan asks the captive audience around the table. "He's the sweetest boyfriend."

"Wait. Excuse me, Jan, but did you just say something about Allen participating in our dance competition?" I ask, wrinkling my forehead as I try to make sense of the partially overheard conversation.

"Why, of course, Rosi. He's a fantastic dancer, taken lessons since he could walk. I have the cutest pictures," she says, reaching for her purse.

"I…I don't need to see pictures. Jan, you *do* realize that the competition is called the Southwest Arizona *Senior* Dancing with the Pros Competition, right? First, Allen lives in Nevada, not Arizona. Secondly, he is not anywhere close to being a senior. He can't participate in our dance competition."

Frank raises an eyebrow at his wife, a bemused look crossing his face as he awaits her answer to me. But he doesn't speak. He's learned the most important ingredient to his successful marriage—silence.

"Rosi," she enunciates, "I *know* that Allen isn't a senior. He'd have been many years younger than *you* should you have chosen to be his girlfriend." She shakes her head slowly back and forth. "What a chance you missed."

Keaton squeezes my knee under the table to remind me not to laugh out loud. "Then doesn't that prove my point? Allen can't participate in the competition we are hosting." I think I hear Karen gasp out loud. Does no one question this lady?

"Rosi, *shut up* and *listen to the woman*," says Brenda.

"Brenda!" says Amos, leaning forward in his chair.

Brenda's cheeks turn a crimson red as she reaches for her water. "I mean, I'm…I'm so sorry, Rosi. I don't know what came over me. I am quite anxious to hear Jan's answer. Silly me. I'm so impatient."

This time I can't keep my laugher inside, but I reach for my margarita as soon as the giggles begin. If I get to see Brenda act like this more often, I'm a huge fan of her relationship with Amos. "Please continue, by all means," I say to Jan.

She takes a deep breath. "As I was saying, *I know that Allen is young,* but he's a professional dancer—"

"Excuse me? But your nephew *Allen* is a professional dancer? I thought he was an exterminator," I say as the waitress delivers our plates of food.

Jan closes her eyes, her hand shaking as she places her napkin on her lap. Maybe I need to tone down my interrogation. It's so fun though.

"Allen *is* an exterminator, one of the best in the country, but he's also been taking dance lessons since he was a wee boy."

Keaton squeezes my knee again.

16

"And I made some calls to the organizers of the Southwest Arizona Senior Dancing with the Pros Competition who agreed to let Allen audition as a pro. Well, I am pleased to tell you that he made it! He will be a back-up professional dancer!"

"A back-up professional?" asks Paula. "What's that?"

Jan clenches her jaw before speaking. "It means that if a professional dancer is unable to perform his duties, then he can fill in. It's actually a more challenging role as he has to learn *all* of the dances, not just one dance."

"That is marvelous news indeed, Jan. He's living the dream."

She doesn't know if I'm being sincere or not as I've tempered my emotions, so she responds only with a small nod of her head. Then the conversation swings back to mundane talk of grandchildren and pickleball and golf outings. I'm actually having a great time listening to the conversations ping pong around the table. Collectively, this group of women and men are very entertaining, and my mom and dad are in their element. It's so nice to know that they are living their best lives after working for so many years. I think the next few months might be really fun. And the only drama will be about who wore the wrong outfit to church or who said an incorrect thing to the wrong person or who fooled around with a married man. Sounds heavenly.

Chapter 3

"Are you ready for today?" Tracy asks as she pops into my office at the performing arts center.

"Ready as I will ever be, I guess."

"I'm looking forward to seeing who shows up."

"Me too. I'm sure glad *I* am not judging who gets to participate in the dance competition. I don't need any accusations of favoritism."

Tracy frowns. "You know I didn't have a choice, Rosi. That was part of the deal. We were selected as one of five retirement communities to provide dancers for the next level of the competition, but we had to create a plan to vet the dancers that would be chosen from our population. We can't let everyone dance. They have standards. Those chosen must have *some* talent. This year, the state level of the Arizona Senior Dancing with the Pros Competition will be televised *and* livestreamed. It's quite an honor to provide locals that will be part of such a wonderful event."

"I know, Tracy. You are the perfect person to help vet the dancers. After all, you are a marvelous dancer yourself." I smile as I lean back in my chair.

"Tap dancing, yes. I am an amazing tap dancer," she beams. "But all of that other fancy stuff? Rumba?

Salsa? Foxtrot?" She shakes her head back and forth. "Nope. Nope. Nope. You *have* to help choose our local contestants."

"Fine," I sigh. "I suppose it should be entertaining. Hey, do you mind if Barley comes in this afternoon? She's been alone all morning, and I feel kind of guilty."

"No more Doggie Care Center?"

"No," I say, sadly. "She's been banned unless I commit to more classes."

"It's their loss, Rosi. I'll stop in with a treat later. Maybe Barley could join us for tryouts in the auditorium? Paula and Officer Lona are also helping us choose the talent."

"Officer Lona?"

"Yeah, she replaced Officer Xena Whitley who quit last week. She's competing at Powerlifting Arizona in Flagstaff. She needed more time to train. She told Officer Daniel she's got bigger goals than solving small town crime."

"Huh. She wasn't the friendliest. I won't miss her. Why is this Officer Lona deserving of a position on the judges' panel when she's brand new to Tucson Valley?"

"That's an easy question to answer. She studied dance at Juilliard before deciding to quit in order to pursue a life of crime fighting—a family tradition that goes back three generations according to Officer Daniel. I haven't met her yet. I'm looking forward to it."

"Sounds promising. At least having a police officer around should deter any threat of crime."

"Don't you dare speak more crime into the universe, Rosi Laruee. Don't you dare."

I laugh. "Fair point. I'll see you this afternoon. I'm going to run home for lunch and pick up Barley."

Barley meets me at the front door of my condo. She doesn't like being alone. If I thought she'd behave, I'd get her a cat to keep her company, but the poor cat would be traumatized. I've seen how she chases Keaton's Ruthie into hiding every time we are there.

My phone rings. I take the call as I stand on the back patio while Barley chases a ground squirrel out of the yard. "Hi, Zak! This call is a nice surprise."

"Hey, Mom. How's it going?"

"Good. Busy. The retirement community is hosting the Southwest Arizona Senior Dancing with the Pros

Competition. Tryouts are today for the locals that will be paired with the professionals."

"Oh my gosh! Don't tell me that Grandma is trying out," he laughs.

I chuckle. "I think I've talked her out of it. At least, I *hope* I've convinced her not to audition. She fancies herself a dancer, but the idea of her dancing scripted dances in a dancing competition rattles my brain."

"It would be entertaining. Remember when Uncle Simon and Aunt Shelly got married? She danced the whole night."

"I remember. I think the wine she consumed was *partly* to blame for her enthusiasm on the dance floor." Barley barks at a bird on the concrete fence between my condo and my neighbor's. "What's new with you?"

"Not too much," he hesitates before continuing. "Well, that's not totally true."

I sit in a patio chair and toss Barley her ball. "What's the matter, Zak?"

"Nothing like that, Mom. It's actually *good.*"

"Then spill the beans, as your grandpa would say. You're raising my blood pressure."

"I was wondering if…I was wondering if I could bring a date to Thanksgiving."

As soon as he's spoken the words aloud, I exhale the breath I didn't realize I'd been holding in. "A date?"

"Not really. That's the wrong word." I listen to him breathe through the phone. "I'm kind of seeing someone, Mom, and I'd like to bring her to Arizona to meet you and the rest of the family."

"Oh, wow. That's…that's really nice, Zak. I'd love to meet your, uh, friend. Does she have a name?"

Zak laughs. "She does. She does have a name. Her name's Lanie."

"That's a nice name. Zak and Lanie."

"Don't make too big of a deal, Mom. And please don't tell Grandma until we get closer to Thanksgiving. She'll advertise the news to her friends as if I've done something earthshattering when all I've done is get a girlfriend."

"A girlfriend," I repeat.

"What's the matter, Mom? Are you…are you *crying?*"

"No, of course not," I say, as I quickly wipe away my tears and try to compose myself. "I was distracted by Barley. She's digging a hole in my garden."

"You'd better take care of that."

"Yes, I should. Thanks for calling. And Zak?"

"Yeah?"

"I'm really looking forward to meeting Lanie."

"Thanks, Mom." He pushes the button to end our conversation.

I reach down to pet Barley who is actually behaving herself quite well, resting at my feet and hoping I will throw her ball again. "Good girl, Barley. Those silly people at Doggie Care Center didn't give you a fair shot. Can you believe it, Barley? Our boy is all grown up. All grown up." I let myself sit there for a few minutes longer, pondering the speed with which life is spinning, and my heart sheds another tear.

Chapter 4

I firmly grip Barley's leash in my hand as we walk into the Tucson Valley Performing Arts Center auditorium. The new flooring on the stage shines, a thing of beauty. What a great update for our center. The memories of Sherman Padowski's demise here a few months ago are quickly fading in the minds of all who enter the room nowadays. It's odd how easy it can be to move on from the tragedy, but one could argue that Tucson Valley has become quite skilled at learning to move on from challenging misfortunes.

"Barley, heel," I command, trying to remember what Dewey had taught in class, but Barley is more interested in trying to get the attention of everyone with her barks. "Barley, stop. Quiet." I slip her a treat from my pocket. That seems to do the trick, but I think *I* am the problem. Like a parent giving in to a wailing child's wants at the checkout when she cries, I'm creating a monster, too, the four-legged kind.

"Hey! There's my favorite dog!" Tracy ruffles Barley's fur and lets Barley lick the end of her nose which is not helping anyone.

"Hi, Paula," I say, waving at one of Mom's good-tempered friends. Paula's dressed for serious business today in a suit jacket and matching black slacks, as Mom would call her dress pants. I always thought *slacks* was such an odd word choice for a pair of work pants since *slacking* is not a skill one would attribute to a commendable employee.

"You must be Rosi," says a petite young woman with a pointy nose and a tight blonde bun that sits high atop her head. "I'm Officer Lona, but you can call me Taylor." She sticks her hand out, and I pause a moment to admire her perfectly manicured nails before returning her greeting.

"It's so nice to meet you. We are happy to have a new addition to the police force."

"I'm happy to be here. I've heard there's been an uptick in crime, and the department was looking to bring some new blood onto the force."

I smile. "Let's hope the days of crime are behind us."

"Really? I love a good investigation. Nothing gets my blood flowing quicker than a good high crime case."

"Huh. That's interes…"

"Rosi!"

I look up to the stage and see my mother excitedly waving at me as if I haven't seen her for weeks though I just saw her this morning when she dropped off a loaf of banana bread she'd made.

"Mom?" I ask, skeptically, seeing her dressed in yoga pants and a long t-shirt that barely covers her behind. "Mom?"

She looks at me with a sheepish grin, throwing her hands out with palms up and shoulders raised, telling me everything I need to know. My mother is trying out for the Southwest Arizona Senior Dancing with the Pros Competition. Before I can respond, she jogs to the other side of the stage to join the group of men and women that are congregating, getting their instructions from Waylon Tolly, the representative from the national Dancing with the Pros Competition. I've had only one meeting with him in person, but that was all the time I needed to get a clear read on his personality and his goals for this event. He's like the energizer bunny but on steroids. The guy won't stop talking, his brain ping ponging with information from one thought to the next, but there is no denying his passion for dance and his love of the Senior Dancing with the Pros Competitions that he helps to organize around the country every year. He is also quite a handsome man with chiseled cheekbones and bright blue eyes that match the blue coloring on the tips of his otherwise blonde hair. The men and women he is speaking with on the stage look very intent on trying to understand everything that he is saying. Even Safia, who is our eccentric matron in Tucson Valley, looks completely entranced by Waylon's very presence. He is much younger than any of the residents onstage, even younger than me, but he commands their respect.

"You didn't know, did you?" Tracy asks as I take my seat next to her at the rectangular cardboard table that will be our judges' table.

"I did not know. That is correct."

"Cheer up, Rosi. Your mom's a great dancer."

"I guess we'll see. Might it be a conflict of interest to have to decide my mom's fate?"

"That's why we are a committee of four," she winks. "Trust the process."

"Here you go, ladies," says Paula as she passes out matching pages of stationery to each of us, lavender paper with a pair of ballet slippers in the corner. The top of the stationery says *Paula's Notes*. I guess we are all Paula today.

"Shall I notate technique or just an overall ability to keep to the rhythm of the dance?" asks Officer Lona as she leans across Paula to ask Tracy her question.

"I think we are mostly looking for that special je ne sais quoi," Tracy says, snapping her fingers loudly in the air."

"Je ne sais…what?" asks Paula as she wrinkles her nose.

"You know, that special *something,* that quality that you can't really describe. You'll know when you know."

"Let me get this straight," says Officer Lona. "You want us to just *know* if a competitor should earn a spot in the dancing competition? And some residents will give us that special je ne sais quoi more than others? That sounds highly unorthodox. We need *criteria*, real qualities and techniques to look for, Ms. Lake." She frowns at Tracy as she speaks, but Tracy doesn't budge.

"Nope. All we need to do is look for je ne sais quoi. You'll see. Trust the process."

I admire her confidence. I pet Barley under the table and sit back in my chair waiting for the contest to begin. Over a dozen men and women stand on the side of the stage listening to Waylon Tolly who looks to be wrapping up his speech as he walks toward a microphone stand on the center of the stage. Ready or not, here we go.

"Hello," Waylon says into the microphone. "Can you hear me out there?" he says a little too exuberantly to the four of us seated at the judges' table as well as a few other people including Mario who has come to support Celia who is trying out today, much to the shock of Mom and all of her friends. I'd heard Mom's side of the conversation with Jan. It went something like this.

"I know. I can't believe it, either. She's so private. Yes, yes. Really coming out of her shell, I guess. Jan, that's not nice. You don't know that. She just might want to try something new. You don't know that she's trying to outshine anyone. And so what if she is? There will only be one winner after...yes, yes. Okay. I'll talk to you later. Bye."

Poor Celia already has a strike against her, and she hasn't even danced a step. In the Tucson Valley Retirement Community, you are either in the clique or you are out. And for whatever reason, it's been determined by the gossiping gaggle that Celia is most definitely *not* in the clique.

"Good, good," Waylon says, snapping me out of my thoughts. "We have a wonderful collection of young friends who are going to dance for us today." Everyone laughs. "They have each chosen their own music. We are going to keep this informal. I'll play the music from my phone which is synced with the speaker system. Contestants will dance for the length of the song, no more than five minutes. And please—no recording. We have music copyright laws to uphold. Our fine judges," he says, waving his hand in our direction, "will converse about the dancers to choose our contestants who will compete at the Southwest Arizona Senior Dancing with the Pros Competition. And please remember," Waylon says as he turns toward the hopeful dancers, "this competition is all in fun, a wonderful promotion for the Tucson Valley Retirement Community. Our organization chooses five statewide retirement communities every year to host our events. Each resident chosen at this level will be paired with a professional dancer. The winner of each of those five events will compete at the state level in the Arizona Senior Dancing with the Pros Competition where one couple will be chosen to go to nationals. It's quite thrilling for Tucson Valley to have been chosen as one of the five Arizona retirement communities to compete this year. It's your turn to shine, my friends. Shine on—with fearlessness and fun! Shine on!"

The dancers erupt into applause, so Tracy, Taylor, Paula, and I join in. It's hard to deny the infectious joy of this man. "Ladies, are you ready?"

"We are!" shouts Paula. "Bring it on!" She unclasps her suit jacket buttons and breathes a sigh of relief that can only be exhaled after releasing the pressure from a tight piece of clothing.

"Wonderful! First up is Ms. Safia Devereaux who will be dancing to Kylie Minogue's version of "The Loco-Motion.""

Safia sashays onto the stage in a characteristic long, flowy skirt, this one with pictures of trains? Ah, it fits the theme. Her normally wild, curly mane is teased up to match the volume of her oversized shirt that hangs off her shoulders with puffy cuffs at her wrists. When the music starts, Safia becomes a wild woman—lots of arm waving and hip shaking—but mixed up in the craze she performs a series of choreographed steps that surprise me. They highlight her ability to keep time with the music and show her creativity. I find myself tapping my foot along to the '80s remake. I don't realize I kick Barley in the process until she lets out a small yap. When Safia has finished, she makes a dramatic curtsy and walks confidently off the stage with her shoulders back and head held high.

"*That* is je ne sais quoi, ladies," Tracy says, grinning broadly as she simply writes Safia's name down on "Paula's stationery" with a big smiley face next to it.

A woman I only know as Lois Stingerman has to be walked to the center of the stage by Waylon. He holds her hand as if she were his elderly grandmother crossing a busy New York City street. When she looks at us, her eyes grow big, and I can see her hands tremble. She must get her hair set at the same hairdresser as Paula because their tight curls are nearly identical. She looks terrified.

"You've got it, honey!" an elderly gentleman yells from the side of the stage where the male participants have gathered.

Lois smooths the front of her simple black dress. When "You Are My Sunshine" pipes through the speaker system, she waves her arms in the air above her head and spins two times to the right before spinning two times to the left. She walks forward and dips her right hip forward, then her left. She mouths the words to the song as she awkwardly bends and walks around the stage, swinging her arms in the air. But not once does she dance. Not once.

Only her presumed partner claps enthusiastically when the song has ended though all of us know well enough to offer polite applause. Lois walks much quicker off the stage than she'd moved at all during her act. Tracy draws a frowny face next to Lois's name.

Brenda dances next, to "All That Jazz" from the musical *Chicago*. To say that the temperature goes up in the room as she dances in her black leotard and fishnet stockings would be an understatement. This rude, self-centered woman has moves—seductive moves—but moves, nonetheless. As she's dancing around a chair she'd brought to the stage as a prop, I watch the men on the stage who are watching Brenda. Amos has a sly smile on his face as he watches his newest amore sway her hips, but George, who's still Brenda's legal husband, scowls so powerfully that I think he's permanently indented a new row of wrinkles across his wide forehead. I can only imagine the thoughts that run through his head.

I peek at Tracy's "Paula stationery" while Celia walks onto the stage. She's simply written the word *WOW* next to Brenda's name. I think that's a fair assessment. Celia's bright red hair shimmers under the lights at center stage, matching her tights she wears under a short black skirt and leotard. I have to give the woman credit for wearing a leotard. She's not as thin and lithe as Brenda, but the way she carries herself is far more attractive and confident. She dances to a rendition of Jeff Buckley's "Hallelujah" in a style that Taylor whispers to us is called lyrical. I'm mesmerized as she moves angelically across the stage. We are so moved that all four of us jump up simultaneously to clap when she is finished, much to the annoyance of the contestants who have already danced and not received a standing ovation.

A succession of unremarkable women dance next, some of whom I've never seen. None of them are noteworthy enough to warrant a name on my "Paula stationery," but I applaud their courage. I check the time on my watch and wonder how much longer we will be here.

Waylon Tolly walks to the microphone. "Wow! Incredible! Ladies, you amaze me, making it very hard for our judges. Let's pause for a moment for a break. I've been reminded by a friend that we might need to allot time for a potty break." He winks at Safia who winks back. "We'll return in ten minutes. Stretch your legs. We are only getting started!"

"I think I'll take Barley out for a break, too," I say to anyone at the table who is listening. No one says anything. Tracy is looking at something on her phone while Taylor and Paula are comparing their lists.

"Come on, Barley."

I am almost to the door that leads outside when someone taps me on the shoulder. I turn around to find the gentleman who yelled supportive comments to Lois during her rather unfortunate dance routine to "You Are My Sunshine." "Oh, hello," I say, smiling and pulling Barley closer to my side so she doesn't jump on him.

"Hi." The man does not smile, his thick-framed, black glasses sliding down his nose. "You're an important person."

"I'm not sure I understand?"

"You're at the table."

"Right. I'm a judge."

"You need to choose my Lois."

"Excuse me?"

"You need to make sure that Lois is a winner."

"Well, Mr.—"

"Foster, Foster Stingerman."

"Mr. Stingerman, I am only one of four judges. I can assure you that we will assess everyone fairly and under the same set of standards."

"Uh-huh." He stares at me so intensely that I have to look away. Plus, the tufts of hair growing from his ears are very off-putting. "Lois is dying. You don't want to die, do you?"

I put my hand on my heart. "I...whoa! Is that some kind of threat, Mr. Stingerman? I'm truly sorry to hear about your wife. You must know that I can't take individual life circumstances into account, though, right? I don't mean to be crass, but everyone on that stage is dealing with some sort of life challenge. We are only here to judge dancing. Nothing more. Nothing less."

"Lois will win. Make it happen. For your own good. Have a blessed day."

I consider letting Barley off her leash to jump on this rude man, but I don't think I can let go of the comfort she is giving me right now.

Chapter 5

"Is everything okay, Rosi?" Tracy asks as she grabs my hand. "You look a bit pale."

"I'm fine. I...Never mind. I'm fine. Thanks."

"Your mama's up next," Paula says too loudly as she reaches across the table in front of Tracy. I am *so* excited for her. Aren't you, Rosi?" When she speaks, I realize for the first time that she's missing a front tooth. How could I have missed that?

"So excited," I say dryly.

Before she can reply, Waylon Tolly walks back to the microphone. "Ladies and gentlemen, we will continue our auditions for the Southwest Arizona Senior Dancing with the Pros Competition. What great fun we are having today!" His silver shirtsleeves shimmer under the spotlight as if he's wearing a shirt made of aluminum foil. "Next up for the judges' consideration is Renee Laruee."

I watch with wonder as my mother walks to the center of the stage. She's replaced the yoga pants with wide-legged pants that flare out at the bottom, a bit reminiscent of MC Hammer's parachute pants though somehow stylish with her black tank top. For an older woman, my mother's arms are well-toned. She looks fantastic. She looks beautiful. The music is instrumental, switching every ten seconds or so from one style of music to another. And every time there is a change, Mom adapts her dance. I recognize some of the moves from my unsuccessful days of dance lessons. Mom had been so happy to sign her little girl up for class much to my chagrin. I was much too impatient to practice what the teachers were trying so patiently to teach me. If I didn't get something right away, I gave up. Mom gave up on my lessons as well. I do recognize the plié from ballet as she bends gracefully at the knees before switching to high kicks in the style of the Rockettes and ending with the hip hop inspired Running Man. Taylor jumps to her feet when the music ends, followed by Paula and Tracy. I hesitate, not because I wasn't thoroughly (and surprisingly) entertained by my mom, but because it might seem like I'm playing favorites. I look more out of place remaining in my seat, so I stand up and applaud too. Even Barley joins in on the fun by barking until we have returned to our seats. Mom waves at me before walking off the stage.

"I told you she would kill it," Tracy says.

"Word choice," I say, not wanting to jinx things. I watch Tracy write RENEE in big letters and circle her name in a purple pen on "Paula's stationery."

The next three women dance with such a lack of passion that their names are easily forgettable except for Dahlia who twerked so hard that she threw out her back and had to be carried off the stage by Waylon until her husband could come and take her to the emergency room. Poor gal. Even Barley looks bored. I text Keaton to see if he can pick her up during his lunch break and take her back to my condo.

"That concludes the women's portion of our competition. Let's take another short break and meet back in twenty minutes to watch our fine men dance." Waylon clicks off the microphone and walks toward the judges' table.

"Hey, ladies," he says, lowering his voice as we lean toward him, his words coming out quickly. "It might be a good idea to use this time to narrow your list to the four young ladies who will be our contestants for the Southwest Arizona Senior Dancing with the Pros Competition. Remember that we have a reputation as a leading dance competition in the nation. We need to provide contestants who are talented in dance, charismatic in personality, and entertaining. I assure you will do the right thing." He winks before walking out of the auditorium without giving any of us a chance to say a word.

"Should we talk in another room?" Paula asks, "So that no one hears us?"

"That's a good idea," says Tracy. "Let's go to my office."

Mario follows us, stopping to pick up a few folding chairs to add to Tracy's office before closing the door behind us. Not once does Mario encourage us to choose his wife, the consummate professional that he is. I pass Barley off to Keaton with a quick kiss for both of them before settling into Tracy's office.

"So, this is easy. Right, ladies?" asks Officer Lona who chooses the comfortable office chair that sometimes serves as the resting area for Barley's dog bed.

"I certainly think so," says Paula, who sits on the closest folding chair. "What names do you have highlighted on your paper, Tracy?"

Tracy holds up her paper, studying her notations and doodles including the frowny face she'd drawn next to Lois Stingerman's name. "My vote would be Celia for technique, Brenda for, uh, *entertainment value,* Safia for creativity and enthusiasm, and Renee for, well, for everything!" She smiles while everyone in the room nods their heads in agreement. "These ladies have je ne sais quoi."

"I completely agree," says Paula, clapping her hands excitedly. "What a fun group of ladies."

"For what we've been offered, I'd have to agree," says Officer Lona. "Though there is a lot lacking in the *technique* department. I suppose that's what the professionals are for," her Julliard bias on display.

"You haven't said anything, Rosi," says Tracy. "What are your thoughts?" She checks her watch.

"I agree, mostly. It's just that…well, do you think we should give Lois Stingerman another consideration?" I look up slowly, afraid of the reception from my question.

"Lois?" says Paula a bit too loudly, making a face of incredulity with her mouth open wide and her gaping hole on display.

"Seriously, Rosi? I thought you were smarter than that. Officer Daniel has spoken so highly of your judgment," says Taylor, her pointy nose looking up at me.

"I know. It's crazy. I just...I just heard that she might be going through some stuff, some big life stuff, and maybe this competition would brighten her spirits."

"We all have big life stuff at our age, Rosi. Don't be ridiculous," says Paula.

"She's right, Rosi," says Tracy. "We could maybe give Lois a job passing out programs or something if you think that'd help?"

"No, that's okay. You're right. Celia, Brenda, Safia, and Mom are the best choices. Let's move on to the men!"

As I close Tracy's office door behind me and walk back toward the auditorium, I can't help but wonder if I've set myself up for more or less problems by not choosing Lois Stingerman. I only hope I can avoid her husband for the rest of the day.

Chapter 6

By the time we have returned to the judges' table, Waylon Tolly is standing impatiently on the stage, swaying his hips from side to side in frustration as if he can send his irritated vibes over us as a punishment of sorts for being late to the table. He taps his watch four times and points at each of us independently before looking at the four men who are standing on the side of the stage, all of the women either having gone home or sitting in the auditorium to watch their future competition.

"I think we're in the doghouse," Paula whispers too loudly as she pats the sides of her hair.

"*Ladies,* thank you for returning. I am afraid we must start with some bad news. Our tryouts have been taking much longer than anticipated, some of us taking advantage of our fine contestants' important schedules. Thus, we have had two gentlemen who had to bow out of the race." He exhales slowly, putting a hand on his heart as he does so.

I think he's being a bit dramatic, but then I realize the real reason for his frustration. There are only four men left in the wings. We need to choose four men to compete in the Southwest Arizona Senior Dancing with the Pros

Competition. But now we have no choice. We will get what we get. Oof.

"Therefore," says Waylon. "The fine gentlemen that remain on the stage are our four male contestants. There shall be no choosing." He hangs his head sadly.

For a moment I think about walking on the stage and giving Waylon a hug.

"Let them dance!" yells Paula.

"Yes! They've prepared. Give them the floor!" says Tracy.

"I'd love to see their performances," says Officer Lona.

"We will stay as long as you'd like," I add, trying to make up for being twenty minutes late though I don't think Waylon Tolly is in any kind of mood to accept our mea culpa.

He looks at the men who all nod their heads eagerly, except for George. "We shall let them dance. Mr. Bob Horace, take your stage." He waves his hand over the stage as he walks away quickly, pushing a button on his phone that pipes Beyonce's "All the Single Ladies" into the auditorium.

Bob wears a black leotard with black athletic shorts. I didn't know they even made men's leotards. He mimics Beyonce's video with a lot of hip thrusts and hand waving as he runs around the stage. He really sells it, and the ten or fifteen people who remain in the auditorium are loving it. Tracy hip checks me so hard as we jump up to support Bob that I'm equally concerned that both Bob *and* I will break a hip before this song is over. But Bob would have my vote no matter how many men competed for a spot.

"Karen is one lucky lady," Paula says more to herself than to any of us at the table. "Mmm, mmm, mmm."

I stifle a giggle as the next contestant walks onto the stage. Mayor Leo Lestman walks with a demonstrative presence as if to say *I'm here*. He is a large man, both in height and girth, but his easy smile erases any chance of intimidation by his size. The Glenn Miller Orchestra's "In the Mood" plays loudly as Leo performs one half of a couple dance, moving freely around the stage going so far as to hold his body in such a way that you can just imagine the lucky girl who'd be twirled and bee-bopped around the stage. Our table starts bouncing up and down as we all tap our feet along on the auditorium floor. We also stand to give a rousing round of applause after his final bow.

"Fantastic," says Taylor. "That man can dance. His technique was fabulous."

Waylon Tolly sits on a stool on the side of the stage. I haven't seen him smile brighter than he is smiling right now. Perhaps his fear of getting four inept male dancers out of Tucson Valley by default has been allayed. "Bravo! Bravo!"

Next up is Amos Aleger, Brenda's new paramour. The rumor mill says Brenda is far from divorced from George, but that hasn't stopped her from flaunting her new *friend*, as she's been calling him. Amos is a hoity toity man as Mom would call those people who like the finer things in life and aren't afraid to show them off. He wears a full suit, perfectly tailored in a black color that matches the peppered color in his hair and mustache. He also carries a cane that he uses to walk to center stage. But it's all a ruse because as sound of Elvis Presley's "Hound Dog" pipes into the auditorium, he throws his cane across the stage, whips off his suit jacket, pulls out a comb to ceremoniously slick back his hair, and pelvic thrusts and dances around the stage much to the small crowd's excitement. I don't even have to turn around to hear Brenda hooting and hollering from her seat. I look at George who doesn't crack a single muscle on his face, betraying all his emotions without one twitch.

"I had no idea the men in Tucson Valley had *those moves!*" Tracy yells over the music.

"Heck, yeah! Bob and Amos have that je neigh spay koi stuff! Don't they, Tracy?" asks Paula.

"They most definitely do!" answers Taylor, "though the technique could use some fine tuning."

There she goes with that *technique* talk again.

"You sly dog," says Waylon as he returns to the microphone to announce the final contestant of the day. "That was quite a surprise—quite a *nice* surprise."

"Heck yeah!" shouts Brenda. The woman has no shame.

"I suppose the unfortunate loss of some of our male contestants due to time *issues,*" Waylon says as he focuses his gaze harshly on the four of us at the judges' table, "hasn't been a problem after all. Every one of our gentlemen has earned his position in the competition. I am most impressed. And now, without further ado, George Riker, please show us what you've got!"

George walks slowly onto the stage, stopping short of center stage. He takes a visibly long breath before turning to face us. He pushes his wire-framed glasses back up his nose and hikes up his blue jeans. Perhaps he's lost a little weight from the stress of the demise of his marriage. I think he could use a belt. And a haircut. Tufts of hair stick out behind his ear which give him a crazy professor vibe.

George remains rooted in place as his music of choice begins to play, an instrumental soundtrack with disco vibes. After what seems like the longest minute in history, George holds his arms out, one hand pointing up and the other pointing down as if he were Barry Gibb in the Bee Gees. Then, as quickly as he'd struck this most unattractive pose, he switches to the robot as he stiffly moves his arms, legs, and neck in the vein of the dance's namesake.

"Make it stop!" I hear someone yell from behind me. *Brenda.*

George looks past us to his wife who continues to humiliate him with her taunts. I can't take it. I nod at Tracy who nods at Paula who taps Taylor on the shoulder and whispers in her ear. We simultaneously stand up and bop to the music and clap along as George slips into the sprinkler, putting one hand behind his neck as he waves the other arm wildly in the air mimicking the motion of a lawn sprinkler. He's quite terrible. The man has no rhythm and no emotion and no stage presence, but he's our fourth gentleman contestant by default. And I'll be danged if I am going to give Brenda Riker any more chance to disgrace the man.

"Thank you, George. Very well then," Waylon says as he turns down the music until George is forced to walk away. He doesn't stop walking when he gets to the edge of the stage, instead continuing until he's left the auditorium altogether through a side door at the base of the stage.

"That concludes our auditions. At this time, I'd love for our judges to please pass up the names of the four men and four women who will be representing Tucson Valley in the Southwest Arizona Senior Dancing with the Pros Competition."

Tracy stands up and walks toward the stage where she hands Waylon a clean sheet of "Paula's stationery," free of her doodles and extra commentary. She motions for the microphone which he hands her. "Thank you, Waylon," she says as she clears her throat. "I would like to thank all our wonderful contestants for participating in the first ever dance competition at Tucson Valley Retirement Community. We are honored to have so much talent here and humbled by your choice to live in Tucson Valley and to share your gifts with all of us. We wish we could choose every single person that auditioned. Please don't let it get you down if you do not hear your name read aloud. Keep being the wonderful you and pursuing your passions wholeheartedly. Thank you." Tracy hands the microphone to Waylon and returns to her seat with a big smile expanding across her face.

"Nice job, boss," I say, patting her knee.

"Thank you, Ms. Lake. Now, for the moment you've all been waiting for. Let's start with the men."

There are snickers in the crowd as everyone knows who the chosen male dancers are, all four of them for the four positions. I look out at the smattering of people that are seated in the auditorium. It's the first time I spy someone out of place, a young man who wears a baseball hat and a pair of sunglasses. If he's trying to blend in, he's doing a very poor job. "Tracy, turn around slowly so it's not obvious, but isn't that guy in the baseball hat Harley Lawrence, the director of the Sunshine Hope Retirement Community?"

Tracy turns slowly and tries to look like she's tying her shoes as she sees Harley a few rows back. "Yes, that's him." She settles back into her chair. "Why do you think he's here?"

"No idea. It looks like he's going incognito on a secret spy mission," I giggle.

"Why must everything be a competition?" she sighs as the competition for which we are gathered together continues. The irony is not lost on me.

"Would the following men please join me onstage when your name is called? The names are presented in random order. And please hold your applause until all the names have been called," he says, looking out over the measly crowd.

"Amos Aleger."

"Woo-hoo! Go, baby!" Brenda yells, clapping so loudly that her applause echoes off the walls of the mostly empty auditorium making it sound as if twenty Brendas are shouting their support of their lover and giving the theoretical finger to their husband all at the same time.

"I'd like to remind the audience to please hold their clapping." He gives Brenda the stink eye. "Leo Lestman."

Leo waves at us as he takes his place next to Amos. "Bob Horace."

"We have to clap when George's name is called because of that barracuda," I whisper into Tracy's ear. Tracy nods in agreement.

"George Riker."

"Boooo…"

"Woo-hoo!" I yell.

"Yes!" says Paula.

"Well done to *all* of our performers," Tracy yells louder.

"Yes, yes!" says Officer Lona as she plays along.

Waylon smiles. He gets it. "Thank you, gentlemen. I have packets with information about practice schedules to give each of you before you leave if you'll hold on for a moment as we announce our lovely ladies who will be dancing in the Southwest Arizona Senior Dancing with the Pros Competition." He looks at the ten women who sit in the audience.

These women have been here for hours. I feel kind of bad as I look back at them from my chair at the judges' table and realize that some of them are going to be crushed—well, at least have a momentary feeling of disappointment. And I know I am partly to blame for their sting of disappointment.

"Hey, Rosi. Rosi, are you listening to me?" Paula whispers across the table.

"Huh? What? Sorry."

"Get that frown off your face, silly girl. These women have had way more heartache in their lives that have taught them not to let a little dance competition get them down," she says as she reads my mind.

"Thanks, Paula."

"Plus," whispers Tracy. "Your mom is going to be *so* excited!"

"Let's get to it!" Waylon announces. "And please remember to refrain from clapping until everyone is announced. The first lovely lady joining us on this amazing journey is Celia Vasquez."

Celia walks quietly to the stage. I look over my shoulder at Mario who is leaning against the wall of the auditorium with an expression brighter than a pot of gold at the end of the rainbow.

"Next, Renee Laruee!"

I silently clap under the table as I watch my mom walk to the stage with an air of confidence that's so attractive. She doesn't look like *just Mom.* Seeing Mom living in her element in Tucson Valley has taught me so much about my parents, and for the first time in my forty years I've seen them as amazing individuals with talents and flaws that humanize them and elevate them at the same time. I'm only disappointed that I didn't view them this way before. I appreciate them so much more for the people that they are, not just because they are my parents.

"Safia Devereaux, please come to the stage and claim your spot in our competition."

"Ugh!" I hear from the audience, and I know exactly who uttered the disgust. I am going to make it my mission to find out why Brenda Riker is such a bitter old lady. It must be awful living in her mind.

"Brenda Riker!" Waylon declares as I am lost in my thoughts.

Brenda has changed into a simple green linen dress. Her high heels click across the auditorium floor as she walks to the stage. A large gold chain hangs around her neck. I try to read the expressions of the three other women who are on the stage as Brenda joins them, but no one cracks. Is everyone afraid of her? She reminds me of that senior girl who liked to terrorize incoming freshmen girls by glaring at them in the hallways.

"Thank you all for joining us today. I've said it before, but I will say it again. The Southwest Arizona Senior Dancing with the Pros Competition is thrilled with our kick-off stop in Tucson Valley. It will be epic." Everyone applauds while I wonder if Waylon is trying too hard to sell the popularity of this show. "I'd like our contestants to stay while I discuss the next steps which will include meeting your professional dancing partners!"

Everyone smiles onstage except for George who looks miserable standing next to Bob and as far away from Brenda and Amos as possible. I don't blame him. Brenda has somehow managed to make her grip of Amos's arm look more seductive than supportive.

"And finally, please give our judges a round of applause for all of their hard work!"

Waylon begins to clap as it spreads throughout the auditorium. We must be forgiven for our tardiness since the men's pool of dancers turned out pretty great except for poor George. Every good competition show needs a silly contestant or two for pure entertainment value though George deserves so much more than being a laughingstock.

He *did* choose to try out, I try to remind myself. Whatever his motivation was, it was *his* choice and *his* choice alone. I imagine he wanted to prove something to Brenda, but he's off to a poor start if his intent is to impress her with his dancing abilities. Poor guy.

"Thank you, ladies, for joining us today. I've had so much fun!" says Tracy as we leave the auditorium.

"What a blast!" says Paula.

"These dancers have potential—most of them," says Officer Lona, "But they all could stand some real dance lessons. I hope the professionals they are partnered with are up to the challenge. I'm off to fight crime now! Stay out of trouble!"

"Is it okay if I head home a few minutes early, Tracy? I need to let Barley out, and I think my brain might be tapped out."

"Absolutely. Nice job today, Rosi. I'm going to try to catch your mom before I leave! See you tomorrow."

As I am starting my walk home to my condo, I check messages on my phone including a text from Zak with a meme of a frozen turkey being used as a bowling ball. Silly boy. I can't wait to see him in Arizona in a few weeks.

As I cross the street to the sidewalk that will take me home, I hear a loud noise growing closer. It happens so fast I can't process right away what is going on as I'm diving for the grass next to the road, forced off the road by a green truck that threatens to run me over.

When the truck has passed, I assess my current situation. My right knee is bleeding so deeply that I think I might need stitches. My arms are scuffed up and will bruise from the impact of my dive to the grass. I see a hand-sized rock on the grass next to my leg, the culprit for my cut knee. I don't want to cry, but it's an unconscious choice at this moment as I sit in the grass trying to process if someone was trying to kill me.

Chapter 7

"Yes, Dan, I'm positive it was a green pickup truck, a bit smaller than Keaton's blue truck," I tell Officer Daniel who takes my statement from the side of the road where I'd nearly been run over. I imagine I should have just walked home and called him since I live so close, but part of me was too traumatized to move. He'd come right away, and I was grateful to see his squad car pull up.

"Did you get an ID of the person driving?"

I shake my head no. "I only saw the truck. I can't tell you who was driving or how many people were in the truck. Thanks." I accept a bandage that he holds out to me from his first-aid kit. "Do you mind seeing if there is any first-aid ointment in there?"

"Sure." He rummages through the box until he finds a tube that he holds up. "Like this?"

"Yes, thanks," I say, wondering if he's really had any first-aid training. I wipe away the dirt on my knee from the ground, apply the ointment, and stick on a bandage though I don't think it's going to do the trick. "I…I."

"Ros…"

When I come to, I am in the back seat of Officer Daniel's police car. "What happened?" I ask, feeling a knot forming on my head.

"Thank goodness! Oh my word, Rosi. You scared me half to death. How are you?"

"I don't know. How'd I get in your car?"

I see a smile form on Dan's face, and I think he sits up a bit taller. "I scooped you up as soon as you hit the ground and got you in the car and buckled into your seat in record time. We will be in the emergency room soon. You must not be a fan of blood, huh?" he chuckles.

"I guess I passed out." I shake my head back and forth, disappointed that I haven't grown out of the days when I'd get squeamish and pass out at the sight of blood. A few cactus spine pricks? I can handle that, but blood oozing from my knee doesn't sit well in my brain.

"In addition to likely needing stitches on that knee, you might have a concussion."

"Lucky me." I lean my head against the window, watching the homes whizz by as Officer Daniel's siren blares though this is not really an emergency. Maybe he's extra worried about me, or maybe he gets kicks out of turning on the siren. No matter, we are pulling up to the emergency room within minutes, and I am relieved.

Keaton appears at my door first, which startles me. "What are you doing here?" I ask, my vision growing fuzzy.

"I called him when we got in the car. You didn't hear me?"

"No."

"Poor thing. You were out cold. Do you need help?" he asks Keaton.

"Nope! I'm good from here. Thanks, Dan—I mean, Officer Daniel."

"Dan is fine. We're friends now."

"Oh, okay, sure. Thanks…Dan."

"Take care of yourself, Rosi. Be cautious. I'm going to start my investigation."

I wave my hand in his direction and lean into Keaton who helps me into the hospital.

"Sorry for messing up your workday again," I say after receiving stitches in my knee from a temperamental nurse who didn't appreciate my audible gasps when she inserted the needle in my knee despite claiming that she'd

61

given me enough anesthetic that I shouldn't be feeling anything. She was wrong.

"Are you kidding me? I've been so immersed in weed control this week, I actually had a nightmare last night that I was attacked by giant weeds. I woke up thrashing my legs in my blankets thinking they were weeds."

I reach for Keaton's hand. "You should have stayed over at my place. Barley would have fought that nasty weed much fiercer than your Ruthie."

He grasps my hand. "You can count on me staying at your condo from now on, at least until the idiot who almost mowed you down is behind bars—if you'll let me."

"I'll let you," I smile weakly. "I don't think Mom and Dad would have it any other way."

"Are you going to tell them?"

"Tell them? Ha! Mom just sent this text." I hold up my phone for Keaton to read.

OMG, Rosi! What happened? Are you okay? What can I do? Have you told Keaton? I'm coming now! Wait! Where am I supposed to go? Are you at the senior center? Police station??????? Call me!

"Wow! Word really does spread fast. I'll text her now and call her after you've had your concussion test. Is that okay?"

"Thanks—again—for always being here. I've never been in so many crazy predicaments in my whole life as I have been since I've been in Tucson Valley. Since my divorce, too, now that I think about it. Huh."

"Maybe you should get married again. I mean, uh, to stop the drama, you know, that seems to follow you."

We are both saved from this awkward turn in the conversation when the doctor arrives for my concussion test.

"Can I bring you another pillow, Rosi? How about some tea? Would you like honey in your tea? Maybe a nice magazine? No, that's silly. You can't read after what you've been through." Mom flits about her living room like a child hunting for Easter eggs, never settling in one spot long enough to actually find what's there.

"Mom, sit down! I'm fine. Please sit down."

Mom drops into her easy chair, but there is nothing easy about this situation. "I'm sorry, Rosi. I just don't understand why someone would want to run you over. It's absurd."

"I know." I lean back on the pillow on Mom and Dad's couch and pull Grandma Kate's green and orange afghan over my body, trying to take a mental break back in time to easier days when the biggest decision was whether or not we were going to make chocolate chip or peanut butter cookies. I'm so grateful that Mom won't travel anywhere without this blanket. Keaton had only agreed to return to work when I'd relented and allowed him to bring me to Mom and Dad's home away from home. I don't think any of them would have been satisfied for me to be alone, even though I'd passed my concussion test with flying colors. And, if I'm being completely honest, I don't know if I will ever stop wanting to be taken care of by my mom when I'm scared or don't feel well, even at forty years old. I don't think I'll admit that to her, however.

Dad walks into the room with a bowl of popcorn, his solution to all of life's ailments. "Thanks, Dad." I set the bowl on the coffee table next to Mom's Betty White bobblehead. Betty nods her head up and down as if encouraging me to express the thoughts that are swirling in my mind. "I had an odd encounter with a gentleman named Foster Stingerman. Do either of you know him?"

"Foster Stingerman?" repeats Dad. "Hmm, I'm not sure that name rings a bell."

"He's wears really thick black glasses and has quite prominent ear hair." I can't remember anything else about his physical look that stands out.

"Oh, we know him, Richard! That's the guy married to Lois. She's in my bridge group. Quite an odd duck, both of them," says Mom. "Why did you ask about Foster?"

"It might not mean anything, but…" I look at my parents who want nothing more than peace and relaxation in their retirement years, and I feel like I've brought them the opposite since arriving in Tucson Valley.

"Spit it out, girl," says Dad as he takes a handful of popcorn from my bowl.

"He's extremely distraught over his wife's health issues. Anyone in his situation would be upset," I try to justify my thinking to myself.

"What are you talking about?" asks Dad.

"What health issues?" asks Mom.

"Lois is dying, Mom. That would make any spouse say—"

65

"Dying?" Mom jumps up from her chair. "That's ridiculous. Lois Stingerman isn't dying." She pulls out her phone and types furiously.

"Who are you texting?" I ask.

"The group."

"Why are you texting your gossipy friends?"

"Because Lois isn't dying, but I want confirmation."

"How do you know? There is *some* information that's sacred, Mom."

"Because she was rattling on and on about her grandkids last week at bridge club, about how she has trips to visit each of them planned at their various universities. Can you just imagine what Zak would think if I showed up at college to hang out with him? Nobody wants their grandmother to visit them at college. Silliness."

"Maybe they are goodbye trips," I say sadly.

Mom's phone dings. "Yep, I was right. Plus, Paula's a visiting nurse volunteer and says that Lois came in for her physical recently and had the best blood pressure reading of anyone that day. They'd laughed together about the fact that nothing was going to take her out."

"Uh, broken confidentiality laws aside, why would her husband tell me that she was dying and that if we didn't choose Lois for the competition, I wouldn't live to regret it?"

"He said what?" I haven't heard my dad yell so loud since a ref called a foul on me in the fourth quarter of our regional basketball game in high school and I fouled out.

"That's it! Did you tell Officer Daniel? Foster Stingerman tried to kill you because you didn't choose his wife for the dancing competition," says Mom. "Can you believe it, Richard?"

"I don't think there's much I wouldn't believe anymore. This community has gone bananas."

"Do you really think so?" I ask.

"Do you have any other theories?" asks Dad.

"Not really. I'll call Officer Daniel, and if you don't mind, I think I want to close my eyes for a bit."

"Absolutely, Rosi. Make that call, and don't worry about anything else." Mom kisses me on the forehead, hands me my phone, and tucks a crocheted Sophia doll from *The Golden Girls* onto my pillow. She picks up her craft basket and ushers Dad and Barley outside where she will work on Blanche. I suppose there are some perks to retirement I will never understand, but if a crocheted family of *The Golden Girls* gives Mom joy, then let the joy flow.

Chapter 8

Today is the first day of rehearsals, and the performing arts center is abuzz with activity. Mario, Tracy, and I cleared out the rooms in the back of the stage, just as we had done to prepare for the '60s Send-off Concert, to make space for costume changes and a casual *hanging out* space for our professional dancers and our local competitors. There will be five days of practice culminating in the Southwest Arizona Senior Dancing with the Pros Competition on Saturday. Each couple will perform two dances for a new set of judges who will choose one local man and one local woman as the winners who will move on to the state level of the Arizona Senior Dancing with the Pros Competition. Unlike the television show, where couples are eliminated one week at a time, we're simplifying the process with a one-and-done performance. Waylon Tolly will be emceeing the Saturday competition along with Kenny Davis, the Tommy Davis Jr. impersonator from our spring concert. After learning that Kenny had been homeless, I'd vowed to hold an event that would support the homeless shelters in the area. Though I never dreamed of Tucson Valley hosting a dancing competition, it will be the perfect event to raise funds for such a worthy cause.

Half of every ticket sold will support the homeless shelters. Kenny was thrilled to be asked to help host the event. His career is on an uptick.

"Rosi, the professional dancers have arrived," Mario says, sticking his head into my office. "Shall I show them to the dressing rooms?"

"Thanks, Mario. I'll greet them. And I really appreciate your help getting this all set up. I know it's going to be a big week."

"I'm not going to lie. I am feeling vibes from the last big event that spanned multiple days here."

"The summer send-off concert?"

"Yep."

"Yeah, I know, but this time there will be zero problems and zero complaints," I say, smiling slyly.

"Considering you were almost run over on audition day, you're off to a great start."

"Since Officer Daniel has ruled out my suspects, we're going with the theory that it was some jerk texting and driving."

"Uh-huh. Do you really believe that?" he asks as he strokes his beard.

"I have to, Mario. Or I'd go crazy."

"Let me know if you need anything," he says as he heads back into the hallway.

Before getting up to face the new challenges of my day, I read through the latest text message from Officer Daniel again.

Foster and Lois have been cleared. They were still in the building when you had your accident. They'd gone for coffee in the café. Plus, Foster drives a Cadillac, not a pickup truck. It seems no one knows anyone that drives a green pickup truck. Sorry, Rosi. Maybe somebody was texting or had a health incident while driving. Be careful just the same.

I slide my phone into the back pocket of my blue dress pants, wipe granola bar crumbs off my blazer, and prepare to meet the professional dancers. Tracy is already greeting our guests when I get to the auditorium.

"Ah, here she is!" says Tracy, beaming. "Rosi Laruee will get you all settled. You're in good hands. I have a small fire to put out in the game room. It seems a leg of our pool table fell off." She shrugs her shoulders, but no one questions her.

"Hello. It is such a joy to have you all here today." I look at the three women and three men who will be making Tucson Valley their home the rest of the week. I don't know if I have ever been in the presence of such a poised, beautiful, well-fit group of people in my life. "Let me show you to your dressing rooms." The group follows me backstage where I direct them to the two dressing rooms, one male and one female, that will serve as their staging areas for the week. "Get settled, and I will show you the practice rooms. You've seen the stage, of course. The local dancers should be arriving soon." The men exit to their dressing room leaving me with the women.

"Thank you," says a woman with short brown hair and a tattoo of ballet slippers on her right bicep. She has kind eyes and an easy smile. "I'm Ingrid." She extends her hand which I take.

"Nice to meet you, Ingrid. I suppose I should have started with introductions. My apologies."

"I'm Emma," says a younger woman with very long blonde hair that she has pulled back into a high ponytail. She wears a leotard and tights, making it clear that she has the stereotypical long and lithe body of a professional dancer.

The introductions continue as I meet Tiffany, the youngest looking of them all, who has red freckles all over her face that contrast with the blue color of her hair. She wears purple glasses and has too many piercing to count, several in her ear and at least two in her nose.

"Wait! Where's the fourth dancer?" I ask. "There should be four of you, I mean, four professional dancers."

Emma and Tiffany share a look. "Didn't anyone tell you?" asks Ingrid as she moves her bag from one shoulder to the next.

"Told me what?"

"Udi twisted her knee while skiing in Colorado."

"Oh!"

"Waylon said you'd brought in a replacement dancer, someone local."

"Really?"

"Hi! Hello! So sorry I am late." Officer Taylor Lona joins us backstage carrying a large water bottle and wearing yoga pants and a sweatshirt that slides off her shoulder. She's the most beautiful police officer Tucson Valley has ever employed.

"Officer Lona?" I ask surprised.

"Hi, Rosi. So sorry I'm late," she says out of breath. "I was chasing a young kid who stole a soda from the convenience store. Not on my watch!" she laughs.

"Why are you here?"

"Didn't Tracy tell you? I'm filling in for the injured dancer. I studied at Juilliard," she says to the dancers, a note of superiority in her voice.

"She didn't tell me, but I'm glad you will be joining us. Ladies, I'll show you to your practice rooms when you are ready." I wonder what Officer Daniel thinks about losing his police partner to a dancing competition for the week.

Due to space issues, the professional female dancers and our lovely gentlemen will practice in the morning, while the professional male dancers and our interesting assortment of local females will practice in the afternoon, at least for the first couple of days. I have a feeling I am going to need to reserve rooms in the recreation building later in the week because something tells me our residents might need all the practice they can get.

I review the list of names on the clipboard in my hands.

>Amos Aleger—Ingrid
>George Riker—Tiffany
>Leo Lestman—Emma
>Bob Horace—Officer Taylor Lona

Waylon Tolly had chosen the assignments. For that, I am grateful. I don't need any more reason for Brenda to be angry with me, and she's going to be none too happy that Amos has been assigned the beautiful woman with the tattoo sleeves and the long legs to die for. Although, truthfully, all of the women are gorgeous.

Bob arrives first with a jovial smile and a pep in his tennis shoes as he practically runs down the hallway when he sees me. "Hey, Rosi! Here I am, ready or not!"

"Hi, Bob. I'm glad you are excited. How's Suzi?"

"She's great—best dog I've ever owned. And Barley?"

"Most trouble I've ever owned," I sigh. "But worth it. I have some news, but I don't want it to deflate your enthusiasm."

"Hit me, Rosi!"

"Huh?" I ask confused.

"Hit me with the news. I can take it." He winks demonstrably.

"Oh, right. The professional dancer you've been assigned to has suffered an unfortunate skiing accident."

"Oh no! Is she okay?"

Of course Bob would think of a stranger before himself. "Yes, she's fine. Well, she has an injured knee, but she's been rendered unavailable for the competition."

"I see. Hmm. Well, that's a bummer. I was really looking forward to dancing, but I understand. I'll be a vocal supporter of the other dancers instead."

"No, Bob. You aren't out of the competition. You're so sweet." I put my hand on his shoulder. "Your new partner if Officer Lona."

"Is that Officer Daniel's new partner?"

"It is. She's a Julliard trained dancer."

"Doing police work in a retirement community?"

"And the surrounding area," I add.

He laughs. "As long as she's friendlier than Officer Daniel's last partner, I'm all in!"

"She is most definitely friendlier than Officer Whitley."

"That guy sure has trouble keeping a partner. Can't be a coincidence that the young female officers are cycling out of his office faster than a javelina running away from my Suzi when we're out on an early morning walk." He shakes his head back and forth.

"Huh. I never thought about that before," recalling Officer Morgan Kelly, Officer Emma Prince, Officer Xena Whitley, and now Officer Lona, all new police officers who have come and gone from the Tucson Valley Police Department since my arrival here nine months ago.

"Anyway, can I show you to your practice room? Officer Lona is waiting to meet you."

"That would be lovely. Thank you."

I collapse into my office chair, closing the door behind me after I have escorted each of the local dancers to their practice rooms. I'm satisfied with the smooth interactions. Tiffany with the blue hair and piercings had been particularly kind to George when they'd met. I imagine she'd heard about his audition. Perhaps this event will be nothing but fun and joy. But as I look at the clock on the wall, I know the minutes are slowly ticking toward the afternoon when the local ladies will arrive, which includes Brenda. And I decide to pour myself a midday glass of wine, a leftover bottle from the '60s Send-off Concert, because I might just need some liquid courage.

Chapter 9

As expected, the afternoon starts with a bang with Safia's arrival. It's the first time I've seen her dressed in anything but her characteristic long, flowy skirt. Instead, she wears a long-sleeved, one-piece leotard that extends from her shoulders to her ankles, in bright purple. She stands out like a plum in a fruit bowl. "Good afternoon, Safia! Are you ready for this new adventure?"

"What's that, Rosi?" she yells.

"I said, *are you ready for this adventure?*"

"Oh, poodles, yes. Quite ready. Sorry about that. Having some auditory issues."

"No problem," I say as I raise my voice a couple of notches. "Ready to meet Stu, your partner?"

"Yes!" she says a little too loudly.

Stu and Sofia will be practicing in the food pantry, a shared space that community members regularly replenish. It operates much like one of those little free libraries where people are encouraged to give and take as needed. Mario has moved all the food items and shelving units to the edges of the room to give enough space for a cha-cha-cha or a salsa, or whatever dance the couple will be learning. Stu has his back to us when we enter the room. I'd met him fifteen minutes earlier when he'd arrived. A small, compact man with a shaved, bald head, and no ounce of fat anywhere on his body, Stu gives off very serious vibes. I wonder if Safia can rub off her charm and fun on him or if he'll be one of the rare people who can return her to Earth.

"Excuse me," I say, as I tap on the wall. "Stu, I'd love for you to meet Safia Devereaux."

Stu turns around without smiling. I can only imagine what he must be thinking when he sees Safia in her purple leotard.

Safia doesn't skip a beat though. "Stuie! I'm so pleased to meet you!" She embraces the man with a hug, pulling his head to her shoulder as she towers above him.

An expression of shock and horror crosses his face when he finally breaks free. I try not to betray my true emotions of merriment.

"My name is Stu."

"What's that?"

"You might need to speak up," I say.

"My name is Stu!" he yells.

"I can see it now! Safia and Stu win the Southwest Arizona Senior Dancing with the Pros Competition! Won't that be thrilling, Stuie?" she beams, not for a minute meaning to insult the man with a nickname he clearly despises.

"I'll leave you to your work! Have fun!" I shut the door behind me before I can get drawn further into this mismatched pairing. I nearly bump into Celia who is standing in the hallway waiting for me. "Oh, sorry, Celia. I didn't know you were out here."

"No problem, Rosi. I'm looking forward to the introduction with my dance partner, please," she says matter-of-factly but not with rude intention.

"Certainly. Come with me."

Celia, dressed in a simple pair of navy blue athletic shorts and an over-sized Tucson Valley t-shirt to cover her bottom, looks ready for whatever her partner has in store for her. Perhaps she would have made a better partner for Stu. At least I can't be blamed for the partner assignments.

Carlos waits in the foyer of the performing arts center where he and Celia will rehearse this week. Every available space means every available space. He's tall, dark, and handsome to the fullness of the definition. But if anyone can avoid being distracted by Carlos's piercing brown eyes, it's Celia. She seems unmoved by such silliness as an attractive man to keep her from achieving her goals.

According to Mario, she is singularly focused on winning this competition.

"Rosi! I am *so* excited!" Mom says as she enters the foyer of the performing arts center. "Hi, Celia. Hello, Mr. Handsome, I mean, hello, Mr. Dancer." She extends her hand to Carlos and blushes as he takes her hand in return. I've never seen my mother blush. It's rather disconcerting.

"Come on, Mom. Let's leave Carlos and Celia to their practice." I pull Mom by the hand and out of the foyer and toward a large supply closet that's normally filled with office supplies that have temporarily been boxed up and moved to the storage under the stage so that it can be used as a dance space. Mario deserves a raise after this week is over. He's also quite adept at finding storage in our building. Perhaps he could make a living being a consultant on one of those home improvement shows, especially the ones that design tiny houses.

Vincent sits on the floor with his legs *criss-cross applesauce* as my friends and I used to say when our legs were flexible to bend so unnaturally. Those days are gone. Too many chunks in my apples. Mom and Vincent will get along marvelously. I knew from the moment I was introduced to the jovial man with the tall, blonde mohawk that his large smile and sparkling eyes would set my mother's nerves at ease and make this a fun event, not a super-serious one. At least Waylon got most of the pairings between professionals and novices correct.

The only introduction left to make will happen on the stage. I'd personally chosen the stage, the actual site of the competition, as the practice space for Brenda. I knew it would make *her* happy and cause *me* less problems. She is already on the stage when I arrive, stretching out on the floor in a paisley print tank-top with matching yoga pants. She's added a fake ponytail extension to her extra blonde hair because I've never known Brenda's hair to be *that long*.

"There you are, Rosi! I've been waiting for five minutes!"

The nerve of me! Five whole minutes. I tighten and untighten my fists before speaking. "Sorry about that, Brenda. I hope you'll find your dance space to be most acceptable. I chose the best room just for you." *Confuse her with kindness.*

"Oh, yes," she stammers. "It's nice to be on the stage. But, where's my partner? Shouldn't he be here by now?"

I look around the room, out over the empty seats that will be full with spectators in a few short days to watch the chosen residents and their dance partners compete for a chance to dance at the next level of the Arizona Senior Dancing with the Pros Competition. Not another soul is in the room but the two of us. "Huh. I'm not really sure, Brenda. I'm sorry." I look at the names on my clipboard.

Safia Devereaux —Stu

Celia Vasquez—Carlos

Renee Laruee—Vincent

Brenda Riker—Joseph

"That's unacceptable, Rosi." She gets up from the floor to look at the names on the clipboard. "Where's Joseph?"

I pull out my phone to call Waylon Tolly when I hear the door at the back of the auditorium opening as someone appears to run toward us, someone out of breath and someone very much not Joseph.

"Allen?" Brenda and I ask at the same time.

"Hi! Sorry I'm late! Aunt Jan gave me notice as soon as she could, but I had to get a few things situated at work before I could get in the car and make the drive from Nevada. I know how important this competition is to you,

Brenda. I didn't want to let you down. The moment I heard that you needed another dancer, I jumped at the…"

"What are you talking about, Allen?" I ask, the oil on his tight black curls glistening under the auditorium lights. He wears running pants and a t-shirt that he must think shows off well-defined biceps because the sleeves are too short, but he only manages to demonstrate that he has two tiny apricot-sized bulges on his arms.

"You didn't hear?" he asks, genuinely surprised.

I wait for his answer, clearly annoyed that I'm missing something important.

"Waylon called Aunt Jan early this morning when Joseph fell ill. I know that Aunt Jan told you I've been chosen as a back-up professional dancer. Don't look so surprised, Rosi."

"I honestly didn't realize that was a real thing. I'm sorry."

Visibly irritated, Allen continues. "Anyway, I said yes, so Aunt Jan was supposed to tell Tracy who would have told you, but I suppose she assumed that once Waylon gave the okay for me to fill in, that she didn't need to ask permission of anyone else."

"Wait a minute," I say, what connection does Jan have with Waylon Tolly?"

Allen's mustache twitches as he laughs smugly. "Uncle Frank's cousin's daughter's friend went to Michigan State with Waylon. Didn't you know? That's why Tucson Valley was chosen as a dance competition site, Rosi. Aunt Jan is so humble, she didn't want anyone knowing that it was because of *her* that TVRC got to host, but that aside, I'm here to save the day."

"You are an exterminator. What dance training do you have? I suppose you have a set of dancing rats at the ready to spin and pirouette upon command." I spit out the words so quickly that a piece of spittle lands on Brenda's arm which turns her unturnable face even tighter.

"Rosi! Disgusting! If Jan can vouch for Allen's dance training, then it's good enough for me. We are wasting valuable time! Go on now and leave us be!"

With a dismissal of her hand, Brenda bids me adieu, and who am I to care if Allen is her new dance partner? It's not like *I* have to dance with him. Singing a duet at karaoke night was enough of a pairing to know that I never want to partner with Allen in anything ever again.

Chapter 10

Tonight, the Tucson Valley Retirement Community is hosting a party for the dancers and the professionals to recognize their contribution to our senior center. There is a general buzz around the area about the dancing competition. Tracy and I have been taking calls from media that stretch all across the state as we are one of only five retirement communities that are providing dancers for the Arizona Senior Dancing with the Pros Competition. And whether or not Allen's assertion that Tucson Valley was chosen because of a distant connection with Jan Jinkins's husband Frank with Waylon Tolly, I don't know, but much as the new technology center brought great recognition to our community, so too will this dance contest.

The last three days have been crazy hectic at work. I've brought Barley with me today, having given up on ever taking her back to doggie daycare after she'd been sent home when she ate my ice cream. I probably could have gotten her readmitted, but I didn't even try. With the retirement community booming and the job responsibilities ever expanding, I've been exhausted in the evenings. Keaton and I rarely do anything but watch television and fall asleep early. I don't have time, energy, or desire to take

Barley to more classes. She is who she is, and I have to live with the consequences. And if that means that I can no longer wear my favorite Illinois sweatshirt because she chewed a hole in it out of boredom during the day, then so be it. Dad says I need to get Barley a friend, but I told him he was crazy.

Currently Barley is sleeping like an angel in her dog bed on the floor under my desk. I have to move my feet to the side since she takes up most of the space. A knock on my door startles Barley only long enough to raise her head and readjust her body. "Come in," I say.

Lois Stingerman stands in my doorway. She wears a simple, blue cotton dress and black flats, but the expression on her face is nondescript.

"Can I help you?" Only when I stand up and move to the front of my desk do I see Lois's husband Foster standing behind his wife.

"I...I'm here to dance," she says softly.

"Excuse me?"

"I'm here to dance," she repeats at an equal volume.

"I don't understand, Lois," I say gently, beginning to think that Paula's information about Lois's health was incorrect.

"She's here for practice," says Foster. "Can't dance without practice," he says, sliding his thick, black glasses up his nose. He should really have those adjusted.

"Uh, Mr. and Mrs. Stingerman, last weekend we chose the local dancers for our dance competition. You were aware then that Lois was not chosen—not this time," I add. "But we very much appreciate you attending our tryouts. You are both valuable members of our community." I smile sweetly, trying to calm whatever is causing this unusual conversation.

"Dance my little bear. Show the mean lady," Foster says, beaming at his wife as if she's the most beautiful creature he's ever laid eyes upon.

Lois looks at her husband but doesn't smile. Instead, she obediently obliges his request as she shuffles her feet to the tune in her head that must be a mashup of a child's lullaby and a jerky hip hop song. I'm embarrassed for her, but she betrays no emotion on her face.

"Yeah! Yes!" Foster claps his hands enthusiastically. "I will wait outside in the truck." Foster turns to walk toward the parking lot, but Lois redirects him the other direction with a gentle squeeze on his shoulders. Foster clears his throat and whistles as he exits the building leaving Lois and me alone in my office.

Lois stares at her black shoes so intently I can't help but stare too. They aren't regular black flats but ballerina-type flats, and they are worn all along the edges as if they've been used daily for quite some time. Barley breaks the silence when she whimpers under my desk as she stretches out. Lois's eyes grow large as she lifts her gaze from her feet to my desk though Barley cannot be viewed from our position in the room.

"What was that?" she asks quietly.

"Sorry! That's Barley. I brought my dog to work. Do you like dogs, Lois?" I ask gently, realizing this is the first time Lois and I have been alone.

"I had a dog once, when Foster and I were first married, sixty years ago now." She inhales and exhales so slowly that I wonder if she's had practice with meditation. Her facial expression is muted.

I reach for Barley's leash on my desk, but Barley barrels out from under my desk before I can leash her, thinking that she's getting a walk. She jumps on Lois, knocking her backward toward the wall before I can stop her. "Barley! No! Down girl!"

But Lois doesn't yell or scold Barley. Instead, she drops to her knees and lets Barley shower her face with kisses. I'm quite impressed as I haven't seen any women in the retirement community who can sit on their knees without cracking, breaking, twisting, or tweaking something. "I am so sorry!"

Lois smiles at Barley and then at me as I leash my undisciplined dog and pull her to my side as Lois spryly stands up, brushing dog hair from her dress. "Don't apologize. I enjoyed every moment of that interaction. Perhaps a dog would be a helpful addition to our home. My daughter has suggested it many times."

I stare at Lois, the woman with the tightly set curls and wrinkles that wind around her mouth giving her an appearance of perpetual unhappiness and wonder why she's really here. "Lois, do you understand that you were not chosen to dance? There were only four spaces available. I'm sorry that we could not choose every—"

Lois puts a hand on my arm. "I know, Rosi. I am a terrible dancer."

"Oh. Okay. You understand then. But I guess *I* don't understand. Foster told me that you are…that you are very…that you…"

"That I'm dying?" she asks, reaching out for Barley as she asks the question.

"Yes. I'm sorry to be so direct."

"I'm not dying."

I loosen the grip on Barley's leash, giving permission for Barley to walk closer to Lois for the attention they both crave. I wait for Lois to continue.

"Foster has dementia. He's in the early stages. Well, not really that early anymore. I guess I can't convince myself that the nasty disease is progressing at a much higher pace than we'd hoped, my daughter and me, I mean. Foster gets fixated on things. And ever since he saw that email you sent everyone in the retirement community about the dance competition, he had it in his mind that I'd dance. Foster loves to see me dance. We met at a dance hall in our teens. He'd said he'd fallen in love the minute he saw me dancing on the floor with my girlfriends, that I'd filled up the space with so much joy and enthusiasm, but I was an awkward, gangly teen whose arms felt longer than her legs and no ounce of rhythm in her body to save her soul. Foster wears those thick eyeglasses for a reason. His vision's been poor his whole life. But somewhere in his mind is a memory of me dancing at that dance hall, and he's convinced that I'm the best dancer in this whole community. He won't let it go unless he sees me dancing on that stage. I'm so sorry." She grabs a handful of Barley's fur and tangles her fingers around it as if trying to garner strength from my puppy.

"I have an idea, Lois." She sits quietly as I explain my plan, and when I am done, a genuine smile passes across her face, so sweet it makes me want to cry.

Chapter 11

"Cha-cha. Cha-cha-cha," Keaton is saying over and over as he sashays around my living room.

I lean against the kitchen island as I watch him dance with himself to a Billie Eilish cover of "Bad Guy." His dress khakis hug all the right places as he gives me an extra wiggle for show as he passes by. "You're a dork," I say though I have to admit he's a dork with moves.

"Perhaps you wouldn't think I was such a dork if I had a partner?" He stops in front of me and holds out his hand.

"I'm a wedding dancer only," I say, putting my hand into his.

"I'll remember that," he says, winking. "Weddings are fun. Maybe we can make it to one someday."

I don't have time to contemplate his meaning as he spins me around on my floor. Barley jumps up and down from the backyard on the other side of the slider door, wishing she could be in on the fun. It's the second spin that reminds me that tile floors and socks don't make for a good dancing combination because when Keaton lets go for improvised solo moves, I keep sliding—straight into my kitchen table which I nail with my side causing me to swear and drop to the ground in a solidly fluid finish.

"I am so sorry, Rosi!" Keaton holds out his hand to pull me up, but my hip and my pride are so badly bruised that I brush it away.

"I'm going to sit here and wallow in self-pity a little longer if you don't mind."

Keaton shuts off the music before joining me on the floor. "You're so cute," he says, kissing me on the cheek before kissing me on the other cheek before settling on my lips for what seems like a very long time, but I don't mind. I don't mind at all. Then he stands up, reaches down, and scoops me up before carrying me to the couch. "I'll get you an ice pack."

But before he can walk away, I pull on the bottom of his t-shirt until he is lying on top of me on the couch. The ice pack can wait.

Tonight's party is being hosted in the Roland Price Technology Center. The building's design was created with intentional purpose for each space and the needs of the retirement community in mind. For events hosted at the performing arts center where the dance competition will take place on Saturday, as well as the sneak peek performance tonight, sometimes a cocktail hour or intermission with drinks will be held in the senior center's foyer, but the space is tight. When creating the tech center, we decided to design a multipurpose room that could house such events as needed from spillover from the performing arts center. The buildings are separated by a short distance on sidewalks that take the guests past Keaton's wonderful landscaping and metal sculptures from the local high school kids as well as the statue that was found at the Corum household with the sentimental poem. Tracy and I fought hard for an area that would fluidly connect the two spaces. Plus, the state-of-the-art virtual reality room is geared up to take its participants salsa dancing in Brazil. The night will be so fun!

I close my office door so that Barley won't help herself to annoying the many people that are going to be filling the building soon. I decide to text Keaton to pick her up when he's done with work and before he comes back for the reception. Bad planning on my part. I hate leaving Barley alone. She hates being alone too.

Next, I find the professional dancers backstage before opening the tech center to the caterers. All six of the dancers (minus Allen and Officer Lona) are lounging in the women's dressing room. Vincent drapes his arm across the back of the old, flowered couch where he sits next to Tiffany with the blue hair. They make a cute couple with his mohawk and her hair, but I don't know if they are a couple at all. Emma laughs at something that Carlos is saying. Even from the doorway, I'm drawn to his deep-set brown eyes. It seems that Emma is quite enamored as well.

Stu sits quietly in a chair in the corner of the room scrolling through his phone. A beanie covers his bald head. Only Ingrid seems interested at this moment in the main purpose for being in Tucson Valley as she stretches her legs for days while sitting on the floor. I've never seen someone look more graceful as they stretch. I bet Ingrid doesn't fart when she stretches. I haven't stretched before exercising *without* that happening for a very long time. Perhaps I should pursue that lactose intolerance theory Mom was telling me about. I remind myself that Ingrid has never had a ten-pound baby.

"Hey, guys!" I wave as way of introduction. "We are so happy to have you all here this week. Thank you for being a part of our community. Before I finalize things for tonight's party, I wanted to check in, find out how things have been going, if you need anything." I tuck my hair behind my ears and straighten my shoulders, something about being in a room full of professional dancers to remind myself that I should work on my posture.

"Everything's cool, Rosi," says Vincent. "Your Mom is killing it." His eyes twinkle as he smiles.

"That's nice to hear. She's having a lot of fun. What about the rest of you?" I look around the room and wonder if I ever looked even half as good as this collective group of people.

"Celia's a delightfully serious dancer," says Carlos. "We're going for it." Emma can't take her eyes off of Carlos as he speaks.

"Not my partner," Stu says, taking a swig of water from his water bottle. "Ms. Devereaux insists that we need more *fun* in our dances to impress the judges. She is a woman that likes to be in charge."

I nod my head in agreement. "Safia's a hoot." Stu does not respond. "Well, uh, most of our residents are motivated by fun at this stage in life. Don't take it personally if she's not as serious about the actual dancing."

Stu crinkles his eyebrows as he squints at me, not appreciating my advice at all. "Any other concerns I can address?" I look quickly away from Stu.

"Not from me," says Emma. "Mayor Leo is awesome, not the quickest on his feet but willing to learn. Perhaps Tiffany has the most challenging job this week."

"Me? Oh, well, George is a terrible dancer, no sugar coating needed. It's obvious the man has zero sense of rhythm, but I've never had a student who tried so hard. We've practiced longer than any other couple in this competition. I'm rolling with it." Vincent casually twirls Tiffany's blue strands through his fingers as she leans against him on the couch.

"I'm more concerned about George's interactions with *my* partner than with his poor dancing," says Ingrid as she stands up, having finally stretched out every perfect muscle in her perfect legs. She's more mature in age than the other professionals. Faint wrinkle lines crinkle around her eyes and mouth as she speaks, much like the lines on my own face that I'm discovering each day as I look in the mirror, but Ingrid will have no trouble aging gracefully.

"With Amos?" asks Tiffany. "Yeah, there's something odd going on between those two men. "When we were working on the group number for tonight, they refused to stand next to each other and never once made eye contact."

I sigh. "I think I can explain that situation. "George is married to Brenda."

"The hot old lady with that goofball substitute for Joseph?" asks Carlos.

"Well, uh…" I had never considered Brenda to be hot, but who am I to argue with a well-defined, attractive male like Carlos? "Yes. She is married to George, but she is dating Amos."

"Ooh."

"Oh!"

"Yikes."

"That explains a lot."

"Scandal in a retirement community. I love it," says Emma as she flips her long hair over her shoulders and stands up to refill her water bottle.

"You have no idea how much scandal we've had in Tucson Valley," I say more to myself than to the dancers. "Which leads me to another matter. There's a woman named Lois…"

Chapter 12

Paula and Karen had organized a crew of people to decorate the multipurpose room for tonight's reception. After greeting the caterers in the foyer under Karen's mural, we walk into the room and are immediately transported into a plethora of dancing cardboard décor. Cardboard jukeboxes, '50s dancers, disco balls, and glittery stars are taped to the wall while crepe paper streamers hang from the ceiling. The budget for décor was low. I can imagine poor Mario having to move his ladder around the room to hang the streamers according to the whims of Paula and Karen, but at least their personalities are much more palatable that some of Mom's friends.

I pull out my phone when it dings with a message.

Any more problems this week?

It's Officer Daniel. I appreciate his checking in on me, but there has not been one more hint of trouble directed at me since my run-in—literally—with the green truck last weekend. Other than a couple of last-minute professional dancer changes, there's been very little about this dancing event that has caused too many headaches. And even the dancer changes were solved quickly with the help of Officer Lona and Allen. I still can't believe that Allen is good enough to dance as a *professional*, but as long as Brenda is happy, then who cares? It's a retirement community dancing competition for bragging rights and a small trophy. Even the one man and one woman chosen from Tucson Valley to compete at the Arizona state level will only be competing for another trophy and the rights to move to the national level. $10,000 is the final reward at nationals, but I highly doubt that any of our dancers will make it that far. I mean, the auditions were fun, but they didn't knock anyone's socks off.

No problems. Thanks.

I set my phone on *do not disturb* and put it into the back pocket of my pants and assess the catering table to ensure that all the food is ready to go after the short dancing demonstration. The burners will keep the pasta and garlic bread warm. Mario has wheeled over enough round tables and chairs from the sports center to seat our dancers and their guests. Tracy's pickleball workshop at the sports center had far exceeded our expectations, and we'd run out of chairs. This time, I'd asked Mario to bring over every last chair though I highly doubt this event will be full as it's not open to everyone in the community, only VIPs like board members and their guests.

"There you are, Rosi," says Tracy. "Keaton was looking for you. He grabbed Barley and took her home."

"Shoot! I wish I'd known he was here." I pull out my phone again and see the missed message.

"Maybe it's time to add Keaton's name to a list in your contacts that go through even when you've activated *do not disturb?*" she asks, smiling accusingly as she leans against a round table. Her curly locks are pinned back today, giving her a sophisticated look that complements her fitted black blazer.

"Maybe." I bite the inside of my cheek as I run through the details of the upcoming event. *Food. Check. Tables. Check. Dancers. Happy check.* "I need to make sure that our local dancers have arrived." I smooth out my own blazer, mine red.

Tracy stops my exit with a gentle hand on my arm. "What's wrong, Rosi?"

"Wrong?"

"You seem distracted."

"Oh. Sorry. I…it's just that this event seems to be going so well. I'm not used to that. Perhaps I'm waiting for the other shoe to drop," I say uneasily.

"Tides have turned in the Tucson Valley Retirement Community, Rosi. Enjoy the calm. I think that this time it's going to last. Plus, those flowers on your desk are gorgeous! You are one lucky girl."

"Flowers?"

"Didn't you see them?"

"No. There weren't any flowers when I left my office."

"Oh, well, sorry to ruin the surprise. I hope…uh, I hope you don't mind, but I peeked at the card. I thought they were from Keaton, but the card was signed WT." She hands me the card.

"WT?"

"Waylon Tolly."

"Oh. That's nice. I'd much rather be on his good side."

"That's for sure. See, Rosi? Things are looking up for you."

"I hope you're right, boss. I hope you're right."

Backstage is bustling with activity when Tracy and I arrive. Vincent twirls my mom around the stage. She looks as happy as a little girl on Christmas morning. Even winning the costume contest at the '80s party on karaoke night didn't make her as happy as she appears to be now. They wear matching blue t-shirts and denim jeans, simple. I like it. Stu stands in the corner of the stage. He's wagging his finger at Safia who is adamantly shaking her head back and forth about something she most definitely does not agree with. It's clear from their attire, though, that Safia does have *some* sway over Stu as his paisley shirt matches her paisley skirt. She looks like a hippy with a large scarf tied around her forehead. The fashions for the actual performance on Saturday will be flashier.

I watch Brenda and Allen dance in step to whatever music is playing in their heads. Allen wears a red jacket to accompany Brenda's blue jacket with an American flag tank top. I'm quite impressed with both of them. At the end of their quiet dance, Brenda pulls a red and white stick, like a giant candy cane, from behind Allen's back and hooks it around his neck pulling him in for a teased kiss before pounding it dramatically on the floor. The crowd will love it.

Each couple will get three minutes to dance as an hors d'oeuvre of sorts for the big production on Saturday that will feature two full length dances, one identical choreographed dance and one free choice dance that a professional judges' panel will assess.

"Hello, Rosi."

I turn around to see Amos Aleger looking dapper in a fitted gray tweed suit, his mustache groomed and ready for the limelight. "Hi, Amos. How has your week been?"

"Fabulous. Just fabulous. I have the best partner," he says, throwing his arm around Ingrid's waist and pulling her closer.

Ingrid smiles but disentangles herself from Amos's grasp. "Thank you, Amos. You are a quick learner. Excuse me, but I need to refill my water bottle."

I watch Ingrid walk toward the dressing rooms, the bright colors of her tattoo sleeve on display under the stage lights. I've never met anyone who has screamed tough chick and elegant peacock at the same time.

"She's pretty fabulous," Amos says as he also watches Ingrid walk away.

"Yes, indeed. Have you had a chance to see Brenda dance too? She's doing a great job."

Amos smiles, recognizing my not-so-subtle attempt to circle back to the current reality as Ingrid is definitely out of his league. "I am very much looking forward to seeing Brenda dance tonight. She is a beautiful woman."

I can't help myself from butting into a situation I have no business asking about. "Have there been any problems with George?" I try to make my question sound as innocent as possible and not that I have any prior knowledge, but I doubt that I am selling it well.

"That old guy? He's such a nerd. *That* is one dance I am very much looking forward to seeing tonight. Poor Tiffany must be beside herself with dread." He laughs heartily, and I decide to stop prying.

"Excuse me, please. It looks like Waylon has arrived. I look forward to watching your dance."

"Take care, Ms. Laruee."

"Thanks," I say as I walk away, wondering if Amos is staring at me the way he leered at Ingrid. Doubtful.

"Hello, Waylon. Thank you for sending the flowers. That was so thoughtful." Waylon unbuttons the top button of his shiny silver shirt and flips open his collar.

"Flowers?" he asks, not stopping to engage in conversation as I follow him about the stage where he keeps stopping to look out into the auditorium as if he's plotting where to place the dancers.

"Yes. I received flowers this afternoon wishing me well and telling me that I was going to *kill it* with my new endeavors. They were signed WT."

"Well, you must have another admirer with my initials, Rosi. I don't send flowers to ladies." With that, he walks across the stage to organize the dancers for a professional picture before the festivities begin.

At 6:00 sharp, Tracy lowers the lights in the Tucson Valley Performing Arts Center as the dancers take center stage. I sit in the audience with Keaton as my date along with about forty other people, mostly board members and close family or friends of the local dancers. Waylon Tolly carries a microphone onto the stage.

"Good evening, ladies and gentlemen. Thank you all for coming here tonight for a sneak peek treat of our wonderful professionals and enthusiastic local dancers."

"That's a slap on your peeps, Rosi," Keaton whispers in my ear. *"Enthusiastic* is the best adjective he could come up with?"

"Shh. Just wait and see," I say. Dad sits on my other side and grabs hold of my hand with nervous excitement as the spotlight lands on Mom and her partner Vincent. They have each added cowboy boots to their ensemble.

"He's quite handsome," Dad whispers into my other ear.

I squeeze his hand. "Nothing to worry about, Dad. Everyone is a professional here."

Just then, Brenda and Allen are highlighted by the spotlight, and Jan begins enthusiastically clapping a row ahead of us.

"Everyone's a professional?" Dad asks skeptically, raising his eyebrows in surprise.

"At least Mom doesn't have to dance with him," I say.

"True."

"And without further ado, let's meet our male dancers and their professionals!" The spotlight moves from couple to couple.

Bob and Officer Taylor Lona wear matching yellow tracksuits with their initials on the back. At least they look like they are going to have fun. George wears a simple tan sweater while Tiffany wears a blue dress that matches her hair. Something tells me that it's not only their appearance that is going to be mismatched. Leo Lestman is dressed like a linebacker in an old football jersey and tights while Emma is dressed like an adorable cheerleader with an extremely high and long ponytail coming from the top of her head. Maybe I should just relax and enjoy this evening. The hard work is done now. It's all up to the dancers—the pros and the amateurs—to entertain. I settle back into my seat as Waylon announces the final couple. Amos wears a Hawaiian print shirt and sunglasses while Ingrid wears a matching multi-colored lei around her neck, giving only partial coverage to her bosom which is covered by a tiny bikini top, and a coordinating straw skirt.

"Dios mío!" Keaton says a little too loud.

"I know," I sigh. "Ingrid is gorgeous." *Did he have to make his feelings about her attractiveness so obvious?*

"No, it's not that." Keaton pauses before looking at me. "Ingrid is my ex-wife."

Chapter 13

The couples begin dancing before I have a chance to ask any questions. I close my eyes and take several deep breaths. Why do I feel like a jealous sixteen-year-old girl? *Why? WHY? Because my boyfriend's ex-wife is a 100 on a scale of 1-10.* I sink deeper into my chair wishing I could disappear inside my red blazer and never come out again.

"Woo-hoo! Yee-haw!" yells Dad after Mom's performance. I don't know if Mom or Dad has a larger smile. He's so proud of her.

"Excuse me a minute," I say to Dad and Keaton. "I need to check on something." I walk backstage to congratulate Mom as George is dancing with Tiffany, if you call what George is doing onstage dancing. It's more like he's bouncing from foot to foot as Tiffany dances around him. But I'm not going backstage to celebrate Mom. I'm going backstage so she can smack some sense into me and knock out this intense ball of jealousy that's sitting in the pit of my stomach right now. I have never needed a "talking to" from my mom more than I need it right now.

"Great job everyone. Congrats! You looked great, Safia! Nice costume, Amos. Looking good, Bob." I pass out compliments as fast as a salesman on the Las Vegas strip handing out coupons. "Gorgeous, Ingrid. Simply gorgeous," I say as I pass the woman who once lay in bed with my boyfriend. Where is my mother?

"Rosi! Hey, Rosi!"

I stop only because I know he won't stop yelling my name until he gets what he wants. I turn around quickly. "What is it, Allen?" I ask, annoyed by this speed bump in my mission to find my mother.

"I was hoping you might be able to help with something."

"Can we talk another time? I'm kind of in the middle of something."

"Oh." Allen studies me for a moment before deciding that my mission must not be all that important. "It will only take a minute of your time. Can I show you my contract?"

"Your what?"

"My contract. Come on, Rosi. Focus. Your signature is on all the contracts for the professional dancers."

"I didn't realize," I say truthfully.

Allen cocks his head to the side and frowns. "You really should read everything you sign, Rosi. It's business 101. I know that because I am a successful businessman."

"Yes, yes, Allen. You're a very successful rat exterminator. Nevada's finest. Cool. Way to go. You're impressive. Can I go now?" I see Mom talking to Celia and Vincent. "Excuse me."

Allen stops me by putting a firm hand on my arm. "Rosi, I need you to *look* at my contract." He hesitates. "Please."

I sigh loudly. "Fine. Show me your problem, Allen."

"Good. Come with me."

I follow Allen into a dressing room I'd set up for the amateurs, a combined space for the men and women, just a place to store bags or purses because there are no costume changes needed for tonight's preview. I look at my watch and realize that we are already late for dinner in the technology center. I hope the burners have maintained proper heat to keep our food warm. I don't need anyone getting sick on my watch.

"Here you go." Allen pulls a single piece of paper from his back pocket and hands it to me.

I grab it hastily out of his hands. The first thing I see is my signature. Only it's not my signature. "Wait a second." I read through the contract, lots of legalese, a hold harmless clause in the event of injuries, etc., etc. Then there's a clause about payment.

"I want to receive the same payment as the professionals. I'm doing the same work—"

I look up at Allen, his red jacket making him look like a circus trainer. All he needs is a top hat to complete his look, his black curls peeking out from under the brim. I realize that one might think the same about me from my own red attire. "Payment? Allen, no one is supposed to be getting payment. Not from the Tucson Valley Retirement Community at least."

"What? This is charity?" His voice fills the room. "Waylon Tolly told me we'd get a hearty stipend."

I don't answer as I read through the contract. *A stipend of $3,000 per dancer will be provided to each professional dancer at the end of the week, November 24, by the Tucson Valley Retirement Community. Should a dancer need to be replaced, that replacement dancer shall receive half of the amount awarded the professionals.*

"That right there, Rosi." Allen points to the part of the contract I'd just read. "See? Half? How can that be fair? I'm doing the same work. Can you fix that, Rosi?"

I look at Allen with wide open eyes before looking back at my signature next to Waylon Tolly's signature. "I didn't sign this contract, Allen. There's no payment for the dancers from Tucson Valley. The payment comes from the national organization, not from us. I have no idea about the financial relationship between the dancers and the national organization."

"No way. That's not true. Waylon Tolly told me himself that—"

The light in the room goes out casting us into darkness in the tiny windowless room save for a nightlight that's plugged into the wall.

"Ohhhhhhhhhhhh. Uhhhh."

"Allen? *Allen?*" I reach for him in the space he'd been moments before, but he's not there. I run to the wall for the light switch, but I run into a chair—hard—sending me sprawling to the floor where I hit my forehead against the hard tile. "Ouch!"

I try to orient myself, reaching out to pull myself up. The first thing I grab is the leg of the person that is standing next to me, but the person shakes me off and runs out the door which I hear click shut. At that moment, the light kicks back on. I look at the floor and scream. *Ahhhhhhhhhh!* I stand up quicker than I've ever moved in my life because the other shoe has just dropped. More trouble has entered Tucson Valley.

The first person who rushes into the room is Stu, not exactly the most comforting sight. "What did you do?" he asks.

I don't realize he is talking to me until I see him look from my horror-stricken face to the body that is lying on the ground at my feet, a knife plunged into his shoulder, and his body writhing in pain. "Don't just stand there!" I hold my aching head. "Call 911!" He rushes out of the room as I drop to the floor beside Allen. "Hold on, Allen. It's going to be okay. Help is on the way."

"Ros…Ros…" Then he closes his eyes, and I say a silent prayer.

Chapter 14

Officer Dan Daniel sits on one side of me and Keaton on the other in the waiting room at the hospital. I've been declared concussion free for the second time this week though my head won't stop pounding. Brenda pats Jan on the back as she paces around the room. My parents huddle across from us along with many of the professional dancers who lounge in chairs, most scrolling on their phones.

"Let me go over this again, Rosi," says Officer Daniel. "You were in the middle of a conversation with Allen about a contract which you dispute having signed, and when the lights went out, someone came into the room and stabbed him in the back."

"Yes," I say weakly, closing my eyes and trying to wish this all away. "That's exactly what happened."

"Why would someone stab Allen?"

"I have no idea."

"Did you hear anyone enter the room?"

"I didn't hear anything. I was focused on that piece of paper. It didn't make any sense. I didn't hear anything, Dan. I didn't see anything. Is Allen…is he…you know?" I wipe at the tears that spill down my face. I don't like Allen, but I don't want him to die. Maybe this *is* all my fault for choosing to *kill him with kindness* instead of *to confuse him with kindness* over my many interactions with him.

"We are waiting to talk with the doctor," he says quietly.

"Dan, Rosi's been through a lot. Can you give her a break—for an hour at least?"

"Keaton, the best time to interview a witness is immediately after the crime, when memories are most fresh." Keaton glares at Officer Daniel. "But I'll get her a coffee. I'll be back."

"Thanks," I say as I lay my head on Keaton's shoulder. I close my eyes, but only for a second as I hear a sweet but assured voice speaking the name of my boyfriend.

"Hello, Keats."

"Hello, Ingrid."

I lift my head. Somehow Ingrid manages to look even more beautiful in a stressful situation. Her leotard hugs everything perfectly. I don't look that tight in all of my expensive Spanx put together.

"I didn't imagine I'd see you again," she says quietly.

"Me neither."

"How is your dad?"

"He's good. And your family?"

"Good. I'm...Rosi...I'm...I'm glad you have Keats. He's a good guy. Let me know what the plans are for the rest of the week. I'm heading back to the hotel. Goodbye."

"Goodbye, Ingrid."

I make eye contact with Mom across the hospital waiting room. She blows me a kiss, yet she has no idea I'd been on my way backstage to tell her about Ingrid being Keaton's ex-wife. Allen's stabbing had put a knife in that conversation. Literally and figuratively.

"That was weird," Keaton says more to himself than to me.

I don't reply as he pulls me closer, resting his chin on top of my head. Any amount of excitement I had once held about bringing this dancing competition to Tucson Valley has evaporated. Maybe I should become a recluse and get a work-from-home job. The less people I interact with, the less chance I'll be a part of another major crime. I sigh out loud and snuggle into Keaton.

But I don't have time to relax as Officer Daniel returns with my coffee. "Rosi, I have some bad news," he says, sinking into the chair next to mine.

I sit up quickly and reach for my coffee. I focus on the warmth of my cup hoping that it will calm my mind before Dan drops his bad news. I look across the waiting room as at this moment Jan is speaking with a doctor. She collapses into Brenda's arms, and the two women stumble toward the wall which catches their fall as they begin to wail.

"Dan? *Dan?* Has something happened to Allen?" I sit up straighter, my body tightening into a ball of knots.

Officer Daniel looks around the waiting room, focusing on Jan and Brenda who are now being surrounded by the other people from the dance competition who have gathered in the hospital in Tucson Valley tonight. Dan sighs. "Come with me, Rosi." He reaches for my hand, and I stand up to follow him, Keaton not asking permission to join us.

He leads us to a private family waiting room and closes the door. "Allen has had a rough night."

"Yes, I recall," I say, annoyed. "Dan, has Allen *died?*" My nerves are pinched every which way.

"Jan has just received that unfortunate news."

"Oh my God in heaven. Oh no. Oh no, no, no."

Officer Daniel grabs my hand again. He doesn't say a word as an odd smile creeps onto his face. "Rosi, stop. Allen's not dead."

"What? Come on, Dan. You just told us that Jan got the bad news, and we saw her reaction. What is going on?" Keaton raises his voice until he is yelling at Officer Daniel.

"Pipe down, Keaton. You're going to blow our cover."

"Cover? What the hell is going on?"

Officer Daniel's creepy smile returns as he raises his eyebrows in an *I'm so clever* manner. "I have a plan," he whispers though we are the only people in the room.

"A plan?" Keaton and I ask at the same time.

"It's kind of complex, so I need you to focus."

Dan is very much enjoying our attention on him, but he is grating on my last nerve. "I am focused," I enunciate with every bit of exaggeration that I intend, restraining myself from executing my strong desire to slap the man across the face.

"Allen is alive," he whispers as he leans close to Keaton and me.

"Thank God!" I say, making the sign of the cross over my heart though I am not Catholic.

"Then why did Jan and Brenda react like that?"

"Oh, well, uh…."

"Dan?" I wait. Nothing. *"Dan?* You didn't have the doctor tell Allen's aunt that her nephew has *died, did you?"*

"I'm sorry, Rosi. I need for everyone to *think* that Allen has died for this plan to work."

"Dan! That's the most horrible thing I have ever heard in my entire life!"

"Oh, come on, Rosi. That's an exaggeration. You've been indirectly involved in countless murders. A little white lie to potentially *stop* future murders isn't as bad as *actual* deaths."

"Why did you lie? What's this grand plan?" Keaton enunciates each of his words, trying to stop himself from punching Officer Daniel in the face. We are both teetering on the edge of rage.

"I've had a long conversation with Allen. He thinks that someone involved with this contract issue is trying to kill him so that they don't have to pay him. If this individual thinks that Allen is dead, then he's safe. He's pretty freaked out. And…"

"And what?" I ask.

"Well, I saw it in a movie once. Everyone thought the victim was dead, so the presumed murderer became careless, went to the 'victim's' house," he says with air quotes, "and the police caught him."

"Are you serious?" I raise my hand in the air. Keaton reads my mind and squeezes my hand tightly, lowering it to his lap. "A movie gave you the idea to lie about Allen's death? All because of a possible dispute of a few thousand dollars? That's absurd!"

A deep red color rises up Officer Daniel's face until it reaches the top of his head which is covered in thinning hair. "I'm going to tell Jan the truth. I needed her reaction to seem realistic."

"Finally, some sense is in that head of yours." I shake my head back and forth over and over, never so disappointed in anyone in my whole life as I am right now by Officer Daniel's policing ineptitude.

"You'll see, Rosi. I'll have this crime solved in no time. Trust me."

"Trust *you?* I think not." I release Keaton's grip on my hand and reach for the doorknob.

"You can't tell anyone, Rosi. Not even your mom. And don't tell Jan you know the truth."

Keaton opens the door. "You'd better tell her right now. Right now!" I say through gritted teeth. We walk out the door which I slam shut for good measure.

Chapter 15

We have gathered all the dancers—the professionals and the locals—into the auditorium at the performing arts center. A full twelve hours has passed since Allen's "death." I've ignored Officer Daniel's orders. If he can lie to most everyone about Allen's death, then I can tell the truth to my parents about his *not death*. Plus, there is no one on this planet I trust with the truth more than my parents. Everyone else in the auditorium is bereft with grief, if not for Allen himself whom most people don't know, then the idea that someone so close to the dance competition would meet his demise so nearby. The whole idea is quite disconcerting. But Officer Daniel has insisted that the competition must go on in order for him to complete his investigation. Tracy and I had been aghast at the idea (even with *me* knowing the truth about Allen). I'd begged Dan to tell Tracy the truth, but he wouldn't budge, and I had to use every ounce of strength I could muster to bite my tongue and not tell her. I'd agreed to lead the meeting with the dancers as she was so broken up.

"Ladies and gentlemen, thank you for meeting with us this morning. I realize that the events of the past twelve hours have put a dark cloud over the Southwest Arizona

Senior Dancing with the Pros Competition." I glance at Jan who is sitting next to Brenda and Amos. None of them show any emotion at all. I imagine that Jan has confided in the two of them about Allen's amazing survival. The actions of most everyone else in the audience range from dabbing eyes to, at a minimum, casting long faces. I take a deep breath as I look at my mother who nods her head in encouragement. "After speaking with Officer Daniel and Waylon Tolly, our representative from the Arizona Dancing with the Pros Competition, we have been encouraged to continue Saturday's show. Our dancers have worked very hard. They deserve to showcase their talents and compete for a chance to move on to the state level. Therefore, practices will continue this afternoon with the show taking place tomorrow evening. Officer Lona will be here, of course, as she is also one of our fine dancers." Taylor raises her hand to remind everyone of her identity as a police officer and that somehow knowing that fact should put everyone at ease, but her presence didn't stop Allen's stabbing. "Are there any questions?"

"Well, there is one obvious question," Brenda says loudly from the audience.

"Yes?"

"My poor departed partner will be unavailable to dance as he is…he is…" Brenda clutches her heart dramatically, and I am fully convinced that she does, in fact, know that Allen is lying comfortably in his hospital room watching old episodes of *The Office* and eating the fast food his Aunt Jan is having delivered to him. He probably thinks he's on a glorious vacation.

"Brenda, perhaps we should talk privately?" I suggest.

"No, Rosi. I demand to know what is going to happen to me." Amos puts his arm around her shoulder and gives her a hug. George sits behind the two of them. For a second, it looks like he is thinking of comforting her as well, but he sits back in his seat when Brenda rests her head on Amos's shoulder.

"Okay then. I suppose everyone would learn about the organization's decision anyway. The Tucson Valley Retirement Community will be sending two female contestants to the state level. One female will be chosen by the judges after tomorrow's performance, and Brenda, you will automatically advance. It's not fair to you that you have lost two partners, Joseph from an illness, and well, Allen…"

"But I've worked so hard preparing my dance!" she says.

I wonder if she'd be so egocentric if she *really* thought that Allen was dead. Probably. "You will still be a part of the opening number. I am sure you can appreciate the challenges that our dancers are facing after this tragic event," I say, daring her to continue to test my nerves.

"I suppose that will have to do then." Amos kisses her cheek, and George looks away. Jan dabs at her eyes, carrying on the ruse.

"Rosi, I don't understand. Why do these things keep happening in Tucson Valley? Two murders in this building alone? I'm devastated," says Tracy as she sinks back in her office chair.

I can't stand the secrecy anymore. This whole situation is so messed up. I close Tracy's office door and sit in the chair across from her. Barley sleeps in the dog bed that Tracy had insisted she buy for her own office. Tracy and I seem to share custody of Barley when we are at work. Tracy needed her more today than me, but I have to come clean. I don't even care if Officer Daniel learns about my confession. "Tracy, Allen didn't die in the building."

"I know that he died in the hospital, but his stabbing occurred in the building, so it's still like he died in the—"

"Stop, Tracy." I exhale. "Officer Daniel told me not to tell you, but I can't stand you not knowing. You're so tortured. I'm sorry."

"What do you mean?" Tracy sits up in her chair and rests her elbows on her desk.

"Allen is very much alive."

"What?"

"I know. It's messed up. Officer Daniel has some stupid theory that he'll somehow be able to draw out the so-called murderer if he or she thinks Allen is really dead—and that Allen will be protected if he actually is in danger, of course."

"Oh my goodness. Oh my goodness. Oh my goodness," she repeats over and over.

"I know. I'm sorry. It was killing me to not tell you, but do you see now? Nobody died in Tucson Valley this week. That's *good* news," I laugh uncomfortably.

"But why would someone want to stab Allen?"

"That's what I wanted to talk to you about. Are you aware that the professional dancers may have signed a contract that says that the Tucson Valley Retirement Community is to pay each of them a stipend of $3,000?"

"What? That's nonsense." Tracy jumps up from her chair which startles Barley who starts barking. "I'm sorry, girl. Go back to sleep." She pets Barley until she settles back into her bed. "That would be eight dancers times three thousand dollars—$24,000! That's absurd. We never would have agreed to something like that."

"$21,000."

"Huh? That's the problem Allen was complaining about backstage. There's a clause in the contract that says that replacement dancers only get half of the stiped. We have two replacement dancers—Taylor Lona and Allen—so that's $21,000. Allen didn't like that distinction."

"Well, it shouldn't matter anyway, Rosi. We never agreed to such a silly contract."

"I know, but my signatures on the contracts say otherwise."

"Your signatures? Rosi, how could you have been so foolish?"

"Thanks for the vote of confidence, Tracy," I say sarcastically. "I didn't sign any contracts. Someone forged my signature."

"Oh. Well. Hmmm." She sits down again. "What do you make of all of this? What does Officer Daniel think?"

"Officer Daniel is pretending that a man is dead in order to draw out the 'killer.' Do you really think he's going to be much help in this investigation?"

"Fair point. What are you going to do?"

"The first thing I am going to do is talk to Waylon Tolly about those contracts."

"Good idea. Rosi, why do *you* think someone stabbed Allen?"

"The guy's a jerk. It's not a stretch to imagine he ticked someone off by saying the wrong thing. But premeditated murder is a stretch. I'm going to talk to him this afternoon—in his secret hospital room—and see if I can figure out something that makes sense."

"I'd go with you, but it sounds like Officer Daniel might be pretty ticked off if he knew that I knew the truth."

"Thanks. If you and Mario could keep the peace here, that would be really helpful. Only one more day, and the dancers will be gone. Hopefully things will stay calm the next twenty-four hours."

"From your lips to God's ears, Rosi."

"Amen."

Chapter 16

"Hey, Rosi. How are you doing?" a timid voice asks as I am leaving the senior center.

"Hi, George. I've been better. How about you?"

"Yeah, I've been better, too," he says, dropping his chin to his chest.

He looks so pitiful I have a sudden urge to hug him which I do without thinking. After a half-second of surprise, George hugs me back. "I'm sorry about Brenda, George. I know what it's like to have a challenging marriage."

"Thanks, Rosi. I just don't understand what she sees in that guy. He's arrogant and cocky and the center of attention—all the things Brenda despises in a person."

Except every one of those characteristics describes herself, I want to say. "Sometimes when people are confused, they make stupid decisions," I offer.

"She shouldn't be confused. No one loves her more than I do. I only left because she was spending so much time on all those stupid appointments. I needed her to wake up—realize that it was me she needed—and not another lip injection or tummy tuck procedure. I wanted her to recognize that I loved her for who *she* was, not some pretend version she's manufacturing with anti-aging procedures. But it backfired. She didn't understand why I left."

"Did you explain things to her, George?" I look at my watch and realize I'm going to miss my opportunity to speak with Allen if I don't leave soon. Officer Daniel has promised me surveillance while I am in the hospital in the event that someone is suspicious about my visit. But he has a hot date with Caliope that he refuses to alter no matter the importance to his investigation. My time with Allen is ticking away.

"I've tried to talk to Brenda, but she's so busy with Amos she won't make time to talk to me."

"Keep trying, George. Good luck." I pat him on the back and make a quick exit.

I wave at Officer Daniel who looks very obvious in his personal car, a solid Toyota Camry. He wears aviator sunglasses and drops down in his seat as if no one can recognize him. He doesn't return my wave. *Nice detective work, officer,* I think. Not.

I deliver a code word to a portly nurse who stands guard at the nurse's station on the fifth floor. Considering that the fifth floor is the psychiatric unit, I'm sure she has much better things to do than babysit an annoying, almost-murdered, exterminator-extraordinaire, semi-professional dancer from Nevada. I don't hold her gruff attitude against her. She seems satisfied that I pose no threat to Allen and unlocks the door to his room.

The television is blaring as I walk into Allen's room. The Real Housewives are yelling at each other. Someone's husband said something to someone else's husband that has put a housewife in a very sour mood. Other than containing a hospital bed with a patient propped up on a pair of pillows, the room looks more like a bachelor pad with McDonald's french fry containers and empty chip bags strewn about on his bed and side table along with not one but three cans of Mountain Dew. "Allen?"

He jumps at the sound of his name, and the bag of Doritos in his hands goes flying across his bed scattering chips on his sheets. "Rosi? What are you doing here?" he asks as he reaches for his cellphone.

"Relax, Allen. Officer Daniel is outside. I gave the code word to Nurse Crabby. I know that you are not dead."

"Oh. Just to be sure, do you mind telling me the code word?" He eyes me suspiciously.

"Vermin Hunter."

A huge smile spreads across Allen's face. "That's a great code word, isn't it, Rosi?"

"Clever," I say dryly. "I imagine you spent some time coming up with that ruse."

For the first time, Allen seems embarrassed by the state of affairs in his untidy room as he begins to collect items of trash within his reach.

"It's okay, Allen. You've had quite a week. I'll cut you some slack—this time. But don't get used to my kindness."

He smiles again and nods his head in understanding. "Thanks. Crazy, isn't it? People think I'm dead. That's wild."

"Truly wild."

"What are they saying, Rosi?"

"Excuse me?" I sit down in a chair next to the window.

"It's not very often that a man can *die* and get to hear what his friends and families say about him. What are people saying?" he asks again.

"Oh, yeah, that's kind of weird. I don't know. I've been focused on the fallout with the dance competition."

Allen's expression changes as he drops his chin to his chest. "But people are really cut up about your *death,*" I lie. "They are really, really sad. You are missed, Allen." It's not nice to kick a guy while he's down even if he's a real tool.

"That's good. I want to be missed."

"Yeah, most people would. Hey, I don't have much time. Officer Daniel's covering my visit with surveillance outside to make sure that I'm not being followed. I have some questions if you don't mind?"

"Go for it. I've told Officer Daniel everything I know, but you and I both know that he's not always the sharpest crayon in a new box."

"Right," I say, though all of the crayons in a new box are the same sharpness I want to tell him. "Do you have any idea who might have wanted to hurt you?"

"Me? No way. I don't have any enemies, Rosi. I'm a fun guy. People enjoy my company. All I can think of is that maybe Waylon Tolly was angry that I was complaining about the terms in my contract offering to pay me only half of the stipend of the other dancers."

"The odd thing about that contract, Allen, is that *none* of the dancers were supposed to be paid, not by the Tucson Valley Retirement Community anyway. The state level competition provides the dancers and pays their salaries."

"But you signed the contract. I don't understand."

"I don't understand either. I most definitely did *not* sign that contract."

"Are you sure?"

"Of course I am sure. I would remember agreeing to give away $21,000 of our hard-earned money. We budget very carefully at the senior center. There was to be no cost to us for bringing the Southwest Arizona Senior Dancing with the Pros Competition to Tucson Valley. In fact, we should *make* money when people buy tickets to the event tomorrow. Also, half of our profit is going to support the homeless shelters in the area."

"Huh. I would definitely talk to that Tolly guy then. He sounds shady."

I nod my head in consideration of this point. "What about the other dancers? How did they treat you?"

"They were all cool. I think that guy with your mom was a bit jealous." He wipes Dorito crumbs off his sheet.

"Vincent?"

"Yeah, that guy. He seemed kind of intimidated when we were practicing the group number for the sneak peek show."

"Intimidated? Are you sure he wasn't *annoyed?"* I can't help myself. Sometimes the words just slip out with no filter. Maybe I have a bit of Sophia from *The Golden Girls* in me.

Allen doesn't sense my mocking tone and keeps going. "Yeah. He pushed Brenda and me to the back of the number in a real brutish kind of way even though we are the far superior dancers to Vincent and your mom. Sorry, Rosi. Not meaning to offend."

"No offense taken. Other than Vincent's *jealousy,* did you have any other problems with the dancers?"

Allen pauses as he looks over my shoulder and out the window into the beautiful Arizona fall day. "That Stu guy's kind of weird."

"How so?"

"Very serious. He has a super eccentric partner in Safia, so you'd think he could chill out a bit." I can't argue with Allen about that. "Maybe George or Amos stabbed me."

I wrinkle my forehead in confusion. "Why on earth would you suspect *them*?"

"Brenda is pretty hot for an old lady, and well, I'm a good package."

Allen runs his fingers suggestively through his dirty black curls, and I have to stop myself from gagging. "Jealousy as a motive again?" I ask more to myself.

"Huh?"

"Never mind. Thanks for your help, Allen. You've given me some things to think about. How are you feeling?" Perhaps I should have begun my conversation with that question. Maybe I'm no better that Allen.

"I'm good. Back's a little sore, but the knife missed all the important things. The jerk must have been a weakling because the knife didn't even go in very far."

"I'm happy to hear that you're going to make a full recovery."

"Thanks, Rosi. Be careful out there."

Chapter 17

Once Officer Daniel is released from my hospital visit to go on his date with Caliope, I drive to the Desert Tumbleweed Inn. I don't tell Dan what I am doing for two reasons. One, he is very excited about his date with Caliope. It's shocking that such a sweet, bright schoolteacher like my friend Caliope would find Dan appealing enough to continue dating, yet I'll have to admit that I've never seen him so happy and relaxed since he began dating her. The second reason I am not telling Dan about my trip to the hotel is that I don't want him to bungle up my interrogation by trying to intimidate my subject with a puffed up police attitude. I'm going to have a simple chat though my intention is very much interrogation motivated.

I recheck my text message from Tracy giving me the room numbers of those involved in the dance competition. Practice has wrapped up for the day, so the dancers are free with their time until the big performance tomorrow. I enter the lobby and take the elevator to the fourth floor. I walk down the hallway to room number 410. I knock. And wait. After a second knocking, Waylon Tolly opens the door. "Hello, Waylon," I say, smiling sweetly. *Confuse him with kindness.*

"Rosi? What are you doing here?"

"I was wondering if you had some time for me to ask you some questions?"

He looks in the hallway as if expecting someone, but he opens the door wider and allows me to enter. It dawns on me that if Waylon Tolly truly is the attempted murderer of Allen, then I might be putting myself in a precarious position as no one knows that I am here. "Excuse me a minute." I pull out my phone to text Keaton.

At the Desert Tumbleweed Inn in Waylon Tolly's room. Asking some questions. Just letting you know. See you tonight. XO

I slide the phone to *do not disturb* because I can imagine that I will receive a very stern text in reply. I'm a big girl. I can take care of myself. I think. I hope. I've been in uncomfortable positions before. My journalist career has prepared me well for all of the odd predicaments I've gotten myself into in the Tucson Valley Retirement Community.

"What can I do for you, Rosi?"

Unlike Allen's room at the hospital, Waylon's room is spotless. His bed is made, his tabletops empty, the only hint that someone has been living here for a few days being an open suitcase on the luggage stand, though from my view, all the clothes inside are neatly folded. Everything about the state of this room matches Waylon's physical persona, crisp and confident and neat. Today Waylon wears a bright gray (Who knew that was such a thing?) button-down, short-sleeved shirt with black dress pants and black shoes—no wrinkles or dog hair anywhere to be found.

"I was hoping you could explain this contract." I pull out the contract that Allen had shown me backstage the night the lights went out and he was stabbed.

Waylon takes the contract from my hand and reads it. "You signed this contract?" Waylon asks more as a surprised question than as an acceptance of fact.

"I most definitely did *not* sign this contract."

"But your signature is on the bottom."

"That is not my signature. And I can prove it if needed. The handwriting isn't even close, whoever decided to forge my signature."

"Ms. Laruee, the…"

"Rosi."

"Rosi, our professional dancers work very hard and put their bodies through a lot to dance every week, especially with novices who sometimes, shall we say, dance out of step, leading to the possibility of injuries to our people. The stipend is extra incentive for our fine dancers to stay with our program."

"But your dancers are paid through the state level of the competition. That was made quite clear when Tracy Lake and I applied for consideration as a location for the Southwest Arizona Senior Dancing with the Pros Competition."

"I am sure you are mistaken," Waylon says, flashing a showy smile with his perfectly white teeth, almost as shiny as his shoes.

"I am not mistaken. I don't know what kind of fast one you're trying to pull on us, but it won't work. This is an illegal contract. Please inform your dancers, or I will be forced to do so myself." I don't wait for an answer as I slam his door shut behind me.

I pull out my phone to call Keaton. "I know. But I'm fine. I'll stop by after work. I've got one more thing to do." I end the call before he can protest further. I know Keaton means well, but I have questions that need answers. Officer Daniel thinks that something fantastical is going to happen with the resolution of this case if people think that

Allen is dead. Plus, he's too enamored with Caliope to consider that his ideas for solving this case are incorrect. He's distracted. The reputation of the Tucson Valley Retirement Community is on the line again, and I'll be danged if I let someone come into my place of work and my parents' beloved community and wreak havoc once again without trying to solve this mystery.

I park my car in Brenda's driveway. I think a surprise visit is the best course of action. I don't want her overthinking anything I might ask her. I check myself in my rearview mirror. Other than a few stray hairs out of place, I'm surprisingly still put together. Not bad for forty. I reapply lip gloss before sliding my phone into my purse and walking to Brenda's door. Her home looks just like my parents' home, brown adobe structure with stark landscaping. The only thing that stands out as wildly different about Brenda's home is that she actually has a garage and not just a carport. Plus, the garage is painted pink—bright pink. There is no mistaking that a Barbie wannabe lives here. I wonder if George protested the paint choice. Probably not. Something tells me that she didn't get too much slack from the HOA board, either, as she seems to maintain a certain level of control over them. I knock on the door. And wait. I knock again. And wait. I see movement through the blinds. I knock again. Finally, Brenda opens the door. Hi, Brenda."

"Rosi? What do you want?" she asks with no ounce of excitement in her voice. She is holding her white poodle Ralphie who barks and bares his teeth at me.

"I was wondering if I might be able to come in and speak with you about a few things."

"I have company," she says as she turns around.

"Oh. I...I won't be long. Perhaps your company might be able to wait while we talk outside? It's a beautiful Arizona today."

Someone opens the door behind Brenda, much to her irritation. "Hello, Rosi. Nice to see you outside of the senior center."

"Hello, Amos. I am sorry to be intruding upon your visit with Brenda."

"Not a problem. Brenda and I have much more time for a visit. You obviously have something pressing to discuss with her." Amos's mustache twitches upwards as he smiles. He is quite a looker. "It's about time for me to call my sister in Phoenix. She doesn't like me to miss our calls."

"Oh? That's nice to have family that you talk to every day." For a moment, I think wistfully about Zak and wish that we lived closer to each other. I can't wait to wrap my arms around him when he arrives for Thanksgiving next week.

"Yes, we are quite close. We have each other's backs so to speak. I'll step outside to make that call, sweetheart," he says, kissing Brenda on her cheek. "You may come in, Rosi. Come on, Ralphie. Let's get some fresh air." Ralphie doesn't budge. "Suit yourself, you silly dog."

"Thank you, Amos."

When Amos steps outside, Brenda points to her couch, an ornate gold color with hot pink accent pillows. "Sit."

"Thanks. Amos seems like a nice man," I say, trying to break the ice.

I think I see a small hint of a smile. "He is very good to me. Much different than George. Amos *gets* me. He doesn't judge—mostly."

"Uh-huh. Of course, George must love you a whole lot to be with you for so many years. He told me that he really misses you."

"Really?" she pats the top of her hair, brushing away errant strands. "That's nice. But times change. I need someone in my life who supports my interests."

Like trying to obsessively overcome the aging process? I think.

"What do you want, Rosi? Did George send you to profess his admiration?"

I smile. "No. I didn't come because of George. I came because of Allen."

"Has something happened to him?" she asks quickly. "I mean, isn't it terrible that someone would kill him?"

I laugh. "Brenda, you don't have to pretend with me. I know that you know that Allen is very much alive."

"Oh. Well, I know because my best friend in the world is his aunt. But, why do *you* know the truth?"

"Because Officer Daniel trusts me and because I was with Allen when he was stabbed. It was pretty traumatic, Brenda."

"What do you want to know?" she sits on the chaise lounger across from me, resting her legs. Ralphie runs out of a nearby room and jumps onto her lap.

"Hello, Ralphie," I say playfully. He growls.

"Ralphie is a good judge of character."

I clear my throat. "Since Allen was your partner this week, I'd love to know if there was anything unusual you noticed. Does anything stand out that might give some suggestion as to who might have wanted to cause him harm?"

"Officer Daniel didn't talk to me about this."

"I didn't know."

"Everyone thinks that I am an airhead—just because of my appearance. But I'm a college-educated, intelligent woman. I have strong opinions, but they aren't always incorrect."

"Of course not," I say. *Stroke her ego.*

"As a matter of fact, I most certainly *did* notice some odd things this week. For one, Allen was quite disrespected by the other professionals. Just because he doesn't travel with them from senior center to senior center doesn't mean that he's less worthy to be in this competition. He filled in for *their* dancer when he got sick. Who doesn't take better care of themselves during dancing season? It's so unprofessional! Plus, Allen was a dance minor in college. He has many performances under his belt. He's a fine dancer, and they should be thanking him for filling in and saving the show. Do you know that not one of those dancers extended their sympathies to Jan when Allen *died?*"

"In fairness, Brenda. He didn't die."

"Well, *they* aren't supposed to know that now, are they?"

"True." At this point, though, I wouldn't be surprised if *everyone* in Tucson Valley knew that Allen was living it up in the Tucson Valley Hospital bachelor pad. "Is there something specific that stands out in your mind other than a general disregard for Allen?"

Brenda sucks in her upper lip, giving me a chance to imagine what she looked like before she started adding filler to her lips. I wish she'd realized she was a perfectly nice-looking woman without all the enhancements, but who am I to judge what a woman should or shouldn't do with her appearance? Maybe I've judged Brenda too harshly. Then I remember her snotty attitude, and I don't feel quite as remorseful.

"I think that Tiffany and Vincent were conspiring against Allen."

"Tiffany? Are you sure you're not just mentioning her name because George is her partner?"

"George? This has nothing to do with George. Tiffany and Vincent have a thing, maybe sexual, maybe not. But there is heavy flirting going on between them at a minimum, and whenever they interacted with Allen and me, they giggled."

"Giggled?"

"Yeah. They laughed at us, Rosi. There—I've said it. I do not take kindly to people laughing at me."

"Certainly not. Did they do anything else besides laugh?"

"Tiffany took a video of us with her phone. She thought she was being sneaky, but I saw her. She probably posted it to her socials. I can't be bothered to track it down."

"I'll look into it. Thanks, Brenda. I'm…I'm really sorry that Allen's unfortunate, uh, stabbing, has taken you out of the couples' dance, but I, for one, am very excited to see you perform with the group in the opening number. And you deserve to move on to the next level. You'll do quite well, I'm sure."

The back door opens, and Amos returns to the living room where he is greeted by Ralphie. "Getting hot out there," he chuckles, picking Ralphie up. Ralphie jumps out of his arms and beelines to my leg where he jumps up and begins barking threateningly. "Are you ladies about done? I was hoping to catch a bite to eat."

"Yes, we are done. Thanks again, Brenda." I shake Ralphie off my leg.

She nods her head but says nothing.

"I'll see you both tomorrow night. I've got to pick up Barley from work. Tracy is likely waiting on me."

"That monster is still at the senior center? No wonder she's still so much trouble. She needs to stretch her legs," says Brenda accusingly.

"Thanks, Brenda. See you tomorrow." I let myself out and wonder why I even tried to compliment that wretched woman.

Chapter 18

"Date night at another senior retirement community?" Keaton asks as he gives me side eye from the driver's seat of his truck. "I'm honored to be chosen for such a fine mission," he teases.

"I'm sorry. Do you ever wish you'd never met me? That maybe life would be easier if you weren't always having to chase down murder or attempted murder leads?" I study his face for an honest answer.

He glances at me before returning his attention to the road. "No regrets, Rosisophia Doroche Laruee. Life is never boring with you in it, and there's no one I'd rather spend my time with, even if it involves sleuthing instead of making out, but I'd opt for making out any time you have free for that too." He winks at me, and I reward him with a kiss on the check.

"Maybe later, tiger."

We pull into the parking lot of the Sunshine Hope Retirement Community, a forty-five minute drive east of Tucson Valley. With a very similar look to Tucson Valley, Sunshine Hope is the second largest retirement community, with TVRC being the largest and more well-respected despite the most recent notoriety with an uptick in murder investigations. I'm grateful that Keaton could get out of work an hour early so that he could ride with me to Sunshine Hope in order for us to arrive by 5:00. I'm really hoping that Harley Lawrence is still in his office at this time on a Friday afternoon.

We pass a thriving row of pickleball courts that adjoin the parking lot. A line of people wait their turn to hit a yellow ball over a net. No one is smiling. They mean business.

In the building, we follow a sign to the director's office. The door is closed. "Shoot! We are too late," I say, frustrated by my poor planning. I really wanted to connect with Harley before the performance tomorrow. "What do we do now?" I knock on the door in hopes that Harley is still working. He is not, but the door pops open upon my knocking. I consider leaving him a note that I was here, but that's stupid. He'd wonder why I didn't just call him rather than make a trip all the way to see him without an appointment. And why *am* I here? Because I'm grasping at straws, trying to investigate anyone that seems out of place in relation to our dancing competition, and there was no reason he should have been in attendance at our auditions. "I think this was a bad idea," I say to Keaton.

"Perhaps not. Rosi, look at his bulletin board." He points to the board that hangs on the wall inside Harley's office.

In the middle of the board is a copy of the flyer I'd made advertising the competition for our residents. And drawn over the flyer is a giant circle with an even bigger X blotting out the circle over the words I'd so meticulously crafted. "What the heck?"

"Your suspicions are right. Someone is very jealous that Tucson Valley is a stop on the Southwest Arizona Senior Dancing with the Pros Competition."

"Wow!" That's when we hear voices coming from the hallway. "Oh no!"

"The closet!" Keaton whispers, grabbing my hand and pulling into the supply closet in Harley Lawrence's office. He pulls the door behind us in the tiny space just as the light from the office seeps under the door.

"Yeah, yeah, I get it," we hear Harley on the other side of the door. "I don't think we need to worry. Tucson Valley is putting a nail in their own marketing coffin with another murder on their premises. Yeah, right? It's a messed up place for sure." Keaton grips my hand as my frustrations with Harley's phone conversation grow stronger. "The ranking of best retirement communities comes out soon. I can assure you that Sunshine Hope will top that list this year. No worries. I've made sure of it. Have a good weekend."

After the sound of shuffling paper and the powering down of a computer, Harley flips off his office light and closes the door behind him. Only then do I let out the breath I'd been holding. Keaton turns the handle of the closet door. "How dare he?" I say as soon as I confirm that the coast is clear. "How dare he try to sabotage Tucson Valley? And what did he mean by *I've made sure of it?* Did he try to kill Allen to give us bad press?"

"That's kind of a stretch, Rosi."

"Of course it's a stretch, but why else would someone try to commit a murder *again* on our property? Every theory is on the table because nothing makes sense. I need to talk to Tracy."

"Okay, let's grab dinner first. I'm starving. Date night, remember?"

"Keats! This is a murder investigation! How do you have an appetite at a time like this? Maybe you should have dinner with Ingrid!" The minute the words leave my mouth I am filled with regret. The jealousy monster has been so perilously near the top of my filter that it was bound to spill out eventually. Perhaps the office of my work competitor was not the most opportune location though.

"Whoa! What do you mean by that, Rosi?"

"I don't know. I didn't mean. I don't…let's go." I reach for the office door and turn the handle, but the knob does not budge. I try again. And again. "It's locked," I whisper. "We are locked in Harley Lawrence's office." I sink to the ground and bury my head in my arms.

Keaton lowers himself to the ground next to me. He reaches his arms around my body and pulls me close. Our silence speaks volumes. I close my eyes and breath in Keaton's aftershave and wonder how I get myself in these situations. Only this time in my life I'm not alone. I have a partner—a partner who accepts me, all of me, flaws and all, and I am grateful. But I also don't want to talk about my jealousy of Ingrid.

"We can't stay here all night," Keaton says against the top of my head.

"I know. What should we do?" I look into the darkness of the room with the blinds drawn.

Keaton walks to the window. It's the kind that opens with a crank. Even opened all the way, there is not enough space for me to wiggle through. "I'm going to break the window. It's the only way. I'll pop out the frame," he says.

"But that's a felony, right? Destroying property?"

"Well, we are already trespassing, so what's the difference? Plus, I think we're only committing misdemeanors. No big deal," he smiles to put my mind at ease, but it doesn't work.

"Great. I guess I'll add to my criminal resume," I say, recalling the revengeful tire slashing of my husband's mistress's tires.

"That's the attitude!" Keaton picks up a rather large cactus bookend from a bookshelf in Harley's office and smashes it into the window, shattering the glass onto the small bushes outside the first floor office. He pushes on the window frame until it budges. "My queen, your rescue awaits."

I accept his hand. "Thank you, my lord." I bow before not-so-gracefully climbing through the broken window. Keaton follows. We do a quick scan of the parking lot before running back to Keaton's truck. It is only when we are in his truck that we both see the video camera in the parking lot.

"That's not good," he says.

"You'd think that I'd remember these things."

Chapter 19

"Rosi, you have no idea how much time you have wasted in my evening. Caliope was *this close* to asking me to stay over. Do you know how long it's been since I have *stayed over* at a woman's house?" Officer Daniel's face has never been so red as it is now nor his voice so loud.

"I'm really sorry, Dan. I didn't know who else to contact. Only someone of your stature could get me out of this scrape." I've decided that appealing to his inflated ego might help to defuse this tension between us.

Officer Daniel takes a long, slow, deep breath. He closes his eyes before opening his mouth. "You are lucky that Officer Margie thinks so highly of me in Benson."

"And she bought Rosi's story about her trying to leave Mr. Lawrence a note in his office when the door closed behind her—and me?" asks Keaton expectantly.

"She's not the brightest officer in the state. She didn't even look for proof of a note, thank goodness, because you didn't leave a note, Rosi, correct?"

"I did not leave a note. But it would be pretty nervy of Harley to argue with me about my motives in his office when it's so clear that he knows that *I* know about his thoughts about the Tucson Valley Retirement Community."

"You still owe for the fixing of that window. Officer Margie would not budge on that point. Also, our force has to offer our services *for free* when they bring in a traveling circus in March. *For free,* Rosi. My time is valuable." He squints his eyes at me in an attempt to look intimidating, and I have to try very hard not to laugh as when he squints, his already huge nose gets pushed out further from his face.

"We both owe you, Officer Daniel. Thanks so much for your outstanding work tonight." Keaton winks at me. He can play the flattery game too.

"Did you gain anything by these shenanigans?" he asks. "Do you have a theory that Harley Lawrence is involved in Allen's attempted murder?"

"I don't know. It's clear he's got a vendetta against the Tucson Valley Retirement Community. I was hoping you could work your police magic and see if Harley had an alibi for Thursday night."

"Right, yes. I can do that. I will do that. Until then, please stay out of trouble. You began the week almost getting plowed down by a truck and ended the week climbing out a window. Can you focus on this dancing competition without any more problems?"

"I can sure try," I say. "Thanks, Dan. I'll see you tomorrow night at the show. I think you're going to be blown away by Officer Lona's performance."

"I hope she can dance better than she can fight crime. She's been rather useless this week."

"Are you sure you don't want me to stay tonight?" Keaton asks as he drops me off at my condo.

I kiss him in the front seat of his truck for a long time before answering. We still haven't talked about my jealousy of his gorgeous ex-wife, and I don't have it in me to have that conversation tonight, so I feign exhaustion though I want nothing more than for Keaton to stay over. "Not tonight. I'm supposed to be at Mom and Dad's for brunch tomorrow morning, and I have a thousand things ticking through my mind in preparation for the dance competition. I won't be good company, I'm afraid."

"I think you're good company all of the time, Rosi." Keaton tucks my hair behind my ear and kisses my neck which makes me tingle from my head to my toes.

"I'll be better company when this weekend is over. I promise. I'll see you tomorrow evening. You're still me date, right?"

"Always, Rosi. I'll always be your date. And don't forget that!" he hollers as I close the door of his truck and prepare to spend the rest of my night eating a quart of ice cream and wallowing in self-pity. I just have to keep Barley away from the ice cream.

Chapter 20

The morning of the Southwest Arizona Senior Dancing with the Pros Competition begins with a bang. Literally. A pounding at my door wakes Barley before me and sends me flying out of bed, reaching for my robe, and tying it around my waist. The banging doesn't stop until I open the door. "Tracy!" I say out of breath. "What are you doing here?"

Her wild curls are even wilder this morning. I wonder if she's even brushed her hair. "You weren't answering your phone."

"No. Sorry. It's on *do not disturb*. I was sleeping in before my brunch at my parents' house. What's the matter? Please come in." Barley greets Tracy with a giant kiss on the arm as she jumps on her, sending her falling to the couch where Barley attacks her with more love. "Barley! Stop it. Sorry!"

"It's okay. You know how much I love Barley's emotional support."

"What's the matter?"

"There's a problem with the money."

"What money?"

"That contract you showed me—the one you didn't sign but had your signature?"

"Yes?"

"The finance department has issued the stipends to the dancers. I ran into Carlos this morning. He was working out in the gym. He went on and on about how much he appreciated the extra money and what a nice surprise it was. Rosi, we are out $21,000! How are we going to explain that to the board?"

"Wait a minute. How did the finance department get those contracts? They aren't even legitimate!"

"I don't know."

"This is all on Waylon Tolly. He's a real snake. I'll call the Arizona Dancing with the Pros board. I'll figure it out, Tracy. It's going to be okay."

"It's not going to be okay, Rosi. The checks have been issued. We can't exactly *take back* the money the dancers have been paid. That would be cruel. The board has such a tight leash on our budget. They are surely going to hold me responsible for this."

"They are going to hold Waylon Tolly responsible for this. I'll take care of it." I put my hands on both of

Tracy's shoulders until she looks into my eyes. "I will settle this matter. Trust me."

She nods her head, but her eyes show fear.

When Tracy has gone, I take a quick shower to get ready for Mom's brunch party. I am not looking forward to the group of gossips spilling the tea on the morning of this important day, but Mom is so excited to have us all over, on *her* big day, that I can't disappoint her.

While driving to my parents' house, I wonder about Waylon Tolly and if he tried to kill Allen to shut him up before he exposed the contract to me. Little did he know he was too late, that Allen had already told me the facts, though he was upset at the perceived slight to pay him less when he should have been content that he was being paid at all, since no one was to receive anything from the Tucson Valley Retirement Community.

When I park in front of my parents' house, their driveway already full, I pull out my phone to check my messages. No one from the Arizona Senior Dancing with the Pros Competition has responded to my inquiry about Waylon's trickery. For now—at least for the next hour—I have to switch from business brain to daughter brain. After walking out on her first breakfast brunch when I arrived in Tucson Valley last February, I owe it to Mom to be fully present for this one, no matter how painful it may be.

"Rosi! You look lovely, dear," says Mom as she pats me on the top of my head like I am a little girl again. "Your dress is adorable. Yellow is a pretty color on you with your dark hair."

"Thanks, Mom." I take her *Golden Girls'* cloth napkins to the table and set them aside the good china that she's using today. It's not her china, of course, as she and Dad are only renting for six months, but she'd been most excited to learn that the owner had purchased a china set at a resale shop and stocked the table settings in their home. *The Golden Girls'* napkins had been a birthday gift from Dad. He'd bought them on Etsy. How techie of him.

The first guests to arrive are Karen and Paula. Paula told me she gave up almost all driving when she was seventeen and backed into a tree, totaling her parents' Ford Country Squire. She'd received a rather harsh tongue lashing from her father that soured her confidence with driving—and, I imagine, with men too—as she's shared some wild stories about her deceased ex-husband. I haven't spent much time with Paula, but she's quickly rising up the pyramid of Mom's friends who I enjoy, but I don't think anyone will dethrone sweet Karen from that top spot.

"Hello, ladies," I say. "Please take a seat of your choice. Mom is pulling out the breakfast casserole as we speak."

"Thank you, Rosi," says Karen. "Are you exci—"

The doorbell rings. "Excuse me for a minute, Karen."

"Hello, Jan. Brenda. Please come in. It's lovely to see you both this morning," I lie saccharinely sweet.

"Rosi, aren't you extra chipper today?" asks Brenda.

"It's going to be a great day," I speak into the universe. "Have a seat, ladies."

Dad left an hour ago to golf with his buddies. I wish I'd taken golf up as a child when he'd tried to introduce me to the game. But, when Simon started beating me at age twelve, I'd decided that golf wasn't for me. I couldn't accept my little brother beating me at anything. I'd give my right arm to be on the golf course right now instead of having breakfast casserole with this collective group of personalities. I really wish they'd all accepted Safia into their group. She's entertaining.

"Here you go, ladies," Mom says as she dramatically places her sausage, green pepper, and cheese breakfast casserole onto a Betty White trivet in the middle of the table.

"It looks delicious, Renee," says Karen as she deposits a napkin on her lap.

"I'm trying a new recipe. I added a bit of onions this time."

"Onions?" shrieks Brenda. "Why onions give me gas," says Brenda. "I can't have gas on the day of the competition. I'll stick to fruit, thank you very much. *You* can take that chance with your digestion if you want to, Renee, but not me."

Karen giggles behind her Blanche napkin while Paula laughs gregariously. "I'll take my chances," says my mother curtly.

"How is poor Allen doing?" asks Karen as she passes the fruit bowl to Brenda.

Jan looks around the table at each of us before recalling that there are no secrets here and that everyone knows that Allen is quite alive. The gossip gang holds few secrets. "He's bored—antsy. He wants to go back to Nevada. There's a young lady he's been courting." She shoots me a look of contempt as if to say, *he could have been yours, Rosi.* "What he'd most like to do, though, is dance with Brenda. That boy was born to dance, I tell you. If he'd not had such an entrepreneurial spirit, he would have taken the creative arts route, but he opted for business school."

"That's completely understandable," says Brenda. "I could tell right away during our practices how adept he is at his dancing craft. You're lucky to have such a multi-talented nephew."

"Indeed I am."

"Although…" Brenda peels her orange and begins to cut the slices with a fork and knife. "Vincent and Tiffany have been awful to him, all that behind-the-back snickering they do. So, maybe he doesn't have the long legs or tan of the professional dancers? He can still keep up. I wouldn't be surprised if one of them tried to take poor Allen out with that knife because of good old-fashioned jealousy."

"You're kidding, right?" I ask as I take a drink of my orange juice. "You don't really think that one of the dancers wanted to harm Allen because they felt threatened by his dancing abilities."

This time Paula has the decency to laugh behind her Sophia napkin though Brenda and Jan can still see her—both giving an evil-eyed look.

"Brenda is not kidding at all, Rosi. Do you really know anything about those dancers? We have no idea what their histories are like," says Jan as she wipes sausage crumbs from her lips.

"So, do you think there could be a murderer performing in our dance competition?" I ask sarcastically.

"Oh my," says Karen. "Should I be worried for my Bob?" Karen holds Blanche over her heart.

"Don't be silly. Vincent has been completely professional in all my interactions with him. It is going to be a perfectly lovely evening. No one is going to harm anyone tonight," says Mom.

"That might not be true. Right, Brenda?" Paula asks as she stares at Brenda with wide eyes.

Brenda blushes. "That was nothing more than a lover's spat, Paula. George and Amos will behave tonight. At least, Amos will be a gentleman. It's not *my fault* that George feels threatened by my relationship with Amos."

"What happened?" asks Mom. She winks at me from behind her Dorothy napkin, looking much like Dorothy in the picture.

Brenda groans. "Amos and I were out to dinner last night having a lovely time when George stopped by our table. He and Amos had words."

"Not very nice words, I heard," snickers Paula. I really am liking her more and more.

Brenda ignores her. "And Amos got a little protective and dumped his water glass on top of George's head."

"Oh my," Karen says again. "That's terribly embarrassing for George."

"It was only water, Karen," says Brenda. "In this weather, I'm sure that what's left of his hair was dry by the time he got to his car."

"If George is so jealous of Amos, do you think he could also have been jealous of Allen's attention to you this week, Brenda?" asks Paula who I imagine is very much enjoying fanning the flames of gossip.

"I'd never considered that theory!" says Jan. She turns to her best friend. "Do you think that George hurt Allen?"

Brenda pushes herself away from the table so abruptly that she almost knocks over the pitcher of water. "Don't be ridiculous. Do you think that I could spend forty years with a man and not know if he were a murderer?"

"Attempted murderer," says Paula.

Brenda glares at Paula. "George didn't hurt anyone. Quit the gossip. He just misses me. He misses me!" Brenda returns her chair to the table.

"Are you crying, dear?" Jan asks as she pats Brenda on the back.

Brenda shakes away Jan's hand. "It's nothing."

"You can tell us, Brenda. We are friends," says Karen.

"Is Amos being too stern again?" Jan asks to which Brenda shoots her the meanest look I have ever seen come from Brenda's face. I had no idea it was even possible for her face to contort in so many directions at once.

"Oops! Sorry!" Jan throws her hand over her mouth.

The loud ding of my phone ends this conversation, much to the relief of everyone at the table. Mom doesn't even look angry that I'd forgotten to silence my phone.

"Sorry!" I pull out my phone to shut it off, but I see Tracy's text with the word *Urgent* and excuse myself from the table.

Urgent. Waylon Tolly has been arrested for fraud. The state police contacted me after the Arizona Dancing with the Pros Committee got your message about the dancers' contracts. Seems he's been pulling a fast one on all the retirement communities this year. The dancers didn't even know about the contracts. He was pocketing all the money himself until this competition when Allen got ahold of the fake contract and threw a fit. That's why Waylon went ahead and submitted the contracts to our finance department. He was hoping to avoid detection for scheming all the other communities. He'd told our dancers that Tucson Valley was "extra grateful" for their performances and wanted to give them a "one-time" stiped. That way they'd never question why the other retirement communities didn't pay them extra too.

Waylon Tolly must have been really angry at Allen for blowing up his plan. Did he try to kill Allen to keep him quiet?

I have no idea. Rosi, we have a bigger problem right now.

What problem?

We don't have an emcee for tonight's competition.

"Rosi? Is everything okay?" Mom asks when I return to the table.

"Yes. No problems. No problems at all," I lie. This is the last group of women that need to be plied with more gossip. "I just have a few things to iron out before tonight's performance. I hope you will all excuse me." I take my dishes to the kitchen and let myself out through the back sliding door before I get peppered with more questions.

Chapter 21

I arrive a half hour before anyone else is due to arrive for tonight's performance. I turn on the lights in the auditorium. In an hour this room will be filled, every seat having been accounted for in ticket sales. Just as we'd had to do for the Sizzlin' Summer Send-Off Concert, Mario and I had added chairs behind the last row. We will have a full house. Unlike that concert which I'd been so excited to see, I can't wait for this night to end. Safia had jumped at the chance to emcee. You'd have thought that I'd asked her to be Miss America with the excitement she exuded through the phone. I'd spent the afternoon writing her lines, simple introductions of each of the couples and the judges though prior experience tells me that she is going to go off script. Kenny Davis called me this morning again to offer his apologies for not being able to step in as emcee. How can I fault the man when he has his first opportunity to perform in Las Vegas? We will still use half of tonight's ticket sales to support the homeless shelter in the community. That noble cause was all because of Kenny reminding us of the need. Maybe someday he'll get his own headliner show.

"Rosi?" Mario calls my name when he sees me standing at the base of the stage imagining all of the possible things that could go wrong up there tonight.

"Hi, Mario."

"I called your name three times. Is everything okay?"

I laugh heartily, and I can't stop laughing. I laugh so hard that I might tinkle myself if I don't get under control. "Sorry, yeah. No. Yeah. No," I smile.

"Rosi, I'm worried about you," says Mario with real concern in his eyes. "Have you been drinking?"

"Only if you count the orange juice from Mom's brunch. No drinks for me today. I'm sorry, Mario. It's been a crazy week, and I have no idea what to expect, so I've decided that if I expect the worst, then maybe I can be pleasantly surprised if a little better than the worst is what really happens."

"That's kind of a rough strategy for getting through life."

"I know. On a different topic, how is Celia feeling about tonight?"

"She is so calm it's eerie. I love to watch her dance, so no matter what happens, *I,* for one, am going to have a wonderful evening."

"That's awesome, Mario. Maybe your attitude will rub off on me. Were you looking for me for a reason?"

"Yes, the photos that Waylon Tolly had taken Thursday night were just delivered in the mail. I thought you might like to see them." He holds out an envelope.

"Perfect. Thanks. I'll put them in my office. Thanks for listening to my mania, Mario. Enjoy yourself tonight."

"You, too, Rosi. Try to enjoy your time with Keaton."

Yes, I'll enjoy every minute of watching my boyfriend watching his long-legged goddess of an ex-wife leap around the stage is what I want to say, but I just nod my head instead before returning to my office.

The office seems so quiet without Barley's panting and snoring under my desk. I pick up a clump of dog hair from my desk chair before sitting down. Brown dog hair isn't an accessory I need on my yellow dress. The first thing I do is check my email. A surprise return address catches my attention. I click to open it.

Rosi, did you get my flowers? It's been a few years, but I was thinking about that day in November when your Grandma Kate died, and I wanted you to know that I remembered. Hope you are doing well.

Wesley

Of course. *Wesley Townsend. Wesley,* my ex-husband sent me the flowers. How dare he? I snatch the flowers from the vase on my desk and throw them in the trash.

Moving on, I open the large envelope that Mario had given me. The first picture is a group shot of all the professional dancers and the local dancers standing with their partners. Waylon Tolly stands in the middle of the group in his silver-studded jacket with a giant smile plastered on his face. What a fraud. I can't believe he'd conned so many retirement communities and pocketed dancer stipends that no one had agreed to pay and that *he* certainly didn't deserve. How could so many communities be deceived and not miss all that money? I also can't believe that Waylon *didn't* have anything to do with Allen's stabbing. Officer Daniel called me on my way to the senior center. Waylon Tolly had been seen on the video camera in the front of the senior center talking with Carlos five minutes before Allen was stabbed. I don't have any idea what they were doing, nor do I need to know. He can be crossed off the very short suspect list, however.

I still find it hard to believe that George would do something so stupid as to try to kill Allen because of jealousy over his pairing with Brenda. If George was going to kill anyone, it would be Amos, right? I shudder at the thought. I don't even want a hint of another murder anywhere near Tucson Valley.

The next set of pictures feature each of the couples, Bob and Officer Taylor Lona in their yellow tracksuits, Leo and Emma dressed as a football player and cheerleader, Amos in his Hawaiian shirt and Ingrid in her bikini top and lei. Jealousy is an ugly look on anyone. I should know, as I spent a better part of a year being furiously angry and jealous of Cara and her relationship with my husband. Wondering what Wes wanted from her that I didn't have in me was a horrible, tormenting feeling. I don't want to feel that way now, and Keaton hasn't done anything to warrant these ugly feelings inside my heart. But I'm human, and sometimes human's think ugly things.

When I get to Allen and Brenda's picture, I do a double take. Brenda is wearing a blue jacket with an American flag tank top underneath. Allen wears a red jacket to compliment the patriotic theme. I remember the red jacket Allen had been wearing because he looked like a circus trainer who was poised to smack a whip on the back of a tiger and make it jump through a hoop. But that's not what I am thinking about right now. Right now, I pick up the jacket that hangs on the back of my chair—the blazer I'd removed on Thursday night before rushing to the hospital with everyone else to check on Allen after he was stabbed, the red jacket that looks just like Allen's red jacket. Maybe it wasn't Allen that the intruder intended to stab when he or she cut the lights. Maybe it was me. Allen and I are practically the same height. What if? What if the person that nearly ran me over after auditions wasn't a distracted driver at all but an intentional driver who was trying to harm me? What if that same person tried to stab me after I remained very much alive after the truck run-in? What ifs jumble in my brain like my clothes on the high heat setting of a dryer. I send Officer Daniel a quick text and walk toward the stage to greet the dancers and to put out any fires that may be simmering.

I find Safia standing in the middle of the stage. She reads from a set of notecards, her new, bright orange reading glasses sitting on the end of her nose. I suppose she thought she needed to follow Waylon Tolly's fashion choices, as she wears a shimmery gold cardigan-like jacket that hangs almost to her shins covering a shiny, long, white skirt.

"Hello, Safia." No answer. "Safia?" No answer. I tap her on the shoulder. She jumps. "Safia?"

"Oh, hi, Rosi!" she yells. "I'm practicing my lines!"

"Safia, are you having some trouble with your hearing?"

Safia's face drops as she studies her gold flats. "You noticed?"

"I noticed, but I don't know that everyone has. Have you seen a doctor? Maybe you have an ear infection."

"No ear infection. The doc says I need hearing aids."

"Oh. That's not a big deal, right?"

"Rosi, if I need hearing aids, then what's next? Soft food? A wheelchair?"

I smile. "Lots of people need hearing aids, Safia. Dad has hearing aids, and nothing slows that man down. So does Paula. You've got lots of life left to live."

"Perhaps you're right. They would certainly make my real estate negotiations simpler. Why, last week I thought an agent offered $10,000 over asking on behalf of his client, and I was thrilled! I'd been trying to sell that house for two months, but he was really offering $20,000 less than the asking price. Ten and twenty both start with the same sound after all."

"Understandable mistake, Safia. I think you should follow up with that doctor. What can I do tonight to help out?"

"Could you stand in the wings—in the same spot? So, if I need anything you can motion for what I'm to do? That might make me feel a little better knowing you're there."

"Absolutely, Safia. I've got your back."

"I look *fat?* That's not very nice, Rosi."

I smile. "I said, *I've got your back!*" I say louder.

"Oh, right. That's much nicer. Thank you!" She gives me a little hug, and I move backstage to check on the dancers.

181

Ingrid is passing out costumes. Everyone is wearing the same costume, only color-coded for partners, to keep things simple. I try to slip past her, but I'm not so lucky.

"Rosi!"

"Hello, Ingrid. Is everything okay? All the costumes look great. Thanks for taking over after Waylon's untimely departure from the program. Thank goodness he'd at least ordered the costumes before his arrest. It's quite an evening. Beautiful weather we are having. I think there are going to be so many peop—"

"Rosi!" She stops my incessant rambling with a gentle hand on my shoulder.

What if Ingrid tried to kill me because she wants Keaton back? Oh my goodness. What is wrong with me?

"Rosi!" she says again. "I want you to know what a pleasure it has been to dance here this week. I know that seems kind of odd considering all the drama, but at least we know that Allen is fine." She holds up her hand to block her next sentence from everyone but me. "We all know he's fine. News spreads fast in Tucson Valley."

"It certainly does," I smile, finding myself begin to relax.

"And on the topic of rumors, a little bird told me that you and Keaton are in a relationship."

"Oh. Did that little bird have a lot of recent plastic surgery by chance?"

She laughs. "Maybe. But I knew already. She only confirmed it. When I saw Keaton sitting by you in the audience on Thursday night, I knew you were in a relationship."

"How did you know?"

"Because I know Keaton's happy face, and his happy face was lit. He's crazy for you."

"Oh." I can feel my face start to blush.

"And I can tell you're crazy about him too."

"I am. I'm crazy sometimes. But I know I'm crazy about Keaton."

"I'm really glad. You've treated us all so kindly this week. Our marriage ended a long time ago. I met my new husband shortly after our divorce, and I always worried about Keaton. I wanted him to find what I have with my husband. And it looks like he's found it—with you."

"Thanks, Ingrid. I know it sounds weird, but it helps to hear this from you. I appreciate it."

"Glad I could help. I guess I should go get dressed. It's almost show time."

"Break a leg!" I say as I walk toward the men's dressing area, and I know I don't at all mean my words in the literal sense. What maturity I am showing. I pat myself on the back.

"Hey, Vincent, are we set for the opening number?" I ask as he walks out of the dressing room wearing a pair of tight black pants (Waylon's choice) and a sparkly green shirt. Mom looks great in green. They will make an attractive couple.

"All set, Rosi. Ingrid took Waylon's silver shirt that matches our style and worked some magic to tailor it to Lois's body. No one will even know she isn't a competing dancer.

"You mean Foster, her husband, won't know. That's the only person we must fool."

"He won't know, and Lois sells her part so effectively that no one will even question why she's dancing in the first number."

"I really appreciate you taking time this week to work with her."

"For sure. My papa had bad memory problems in the last couple years of his life. He even forgot my name. It was heartbreaking. If seeing his wife dance on that stage gives this guy happiness, even if only for a short time, it's worth it. I'm honored to have been a part of it."

"Thanks, Vincent. Have fun tonight."

"Hey, Rosi! Your mom has a real chance of winning this thing."

"I guess we'll see soon enough. Have fun!"

"Rosi, I have to talk to you right away. I have to talk to you now!" Brenda's voice is panicky. She adjusts her flashy pink shirt that keeps falling off her shoulder.

"I can get you a safety pin for that if you'd like."

"Not now. There is no time for alterations." She grabs my hand and pulls me toward the tiny storage closet off the side of the stage.

But just as quickly as she pulls me toward the room, she drops my hand and starts patting her hair in a haphazard way and saying, "Yes, *Rosi*. I am quite ready for my dance. Why would you even ask me that? Don't be silly!" she yells.

"Brenda, I don't under—"

"Amos!" Brenda throws her arms around Amos's neck. "Amos, you are so handsome in orange. You look sweet as a peach. I could eat you up!" she gushes.

"I...I..."

"Hello, Rosi. You should have asked for a shimmery yellow shirt since that seems to be your favorite color. Then you'd match all the dancers," says Amos.

"That would have been a great idea," I say, looking from Amos to Brenda and back again.

"I was just telling Rosi that I am excited to dance with Stu tonight since Safia's stepped into Waylon Tolly's role. He's told me that I am much more serious than Safia. What good fortune he has—ha, ha, ha," she laughs uneasily.

"I'm glad that it's worked out for you, Brenda. But remember, as I told you after Allen's unfortunate, well, after he was stabbed, you were given a golden ticket of sorts to advance to the state competition. It's the fair thing to do. There will be two women from the Tucson Valley Retirement Community advancing."

"Yes, dear. That's so kind of you."

"Good luck, my sweetie." Amos bends down and plants a long kiss on Brenda's lips. "Good luck tonight to you as well, Rosi."

"Thank you, Amos. I look forward to watching you dance."

George, in a neon purple shirt, sits on the stage watching Brenda and me. He looks so sad. "Brenda, what is going on?" I ask when Amos has entered the men's dressing room.

"Rosi, I don't know. He might be watching—"

"Who might be watching, Brenda? Amos?" I whisper.

She nods her head quickly.

"Can you be quick?"

She nods her head again.

Without opening her mouth more than a half inch, Brenda manages to convey her message. She'd wanted Amos to drive tonight because her car had been making a clicking sound, so she opened her garage where he'd been parking. In fact, he hadn't spent a single night at his own place since arriving in Tucson Valley. He'd been with Brenda since the very first night. I couldn't help but cast judgement. When she'd opened the garage to pull out his truck, she'd seen a large dent in the front bumper. That's when she'd said it all clicked and she remembered Mom telling her that it had been a green pickup truck that had tried to run me over earlier in the week. She didn't know what it meant, but she wanted to warn me, and she wanted me to know that she'd be staying with Jan until everything was figured out because she was too afraid to stay alone. Also, she'd decided to drive her car even with the clicking sound.

I don't even have time to thank her as she starts fake yelling at me when she spies Amos again—about not having costumes that fit properly or something like that. Instead, I grab her hand and squeeze it hard. I hope she understands that *I* understand and appreciate her information.

My head is spinning with questions, but I don't have time to do anything but move to my spot on the side of the stage because it's 7:00. The show must go on.

Chapter 22

"Welcome, ladies and gentlemen, to the Southwest Arizona Senior Dancing with the Pros Competition where one female and one male resident will be chosen to compete at the state level. My name is Safia Devereux, and I will be your host for the evening's festivities!" she yells into the microphone.

When she looks at me, I hold out both of my hands and lower them. She takes my cue and reduces the volume of her voice. Poor thing just needs to get those hearing aids already.

"I'd like to introduce our panel of judges that will choose our winning dancers. Gerty Wilems is a former dance instructor at Arizona State University." Gerty stands and waves at the crowd. "Isn't she the cutest little thing you've ever seen?" coos Safia. "Love that long skirt, girl!" The crowd laughs, but Gerty does not. "And next we have Bradley Pitt Cooper. I'm kidding, y'all. Oh, poodles, I'm silly tonight. But I think we can all agree that Bradley Pots is as high a caliber actor as any other fine man named Brad. Bradley Potts comes to us all the way from Los Angeles, California where he stars in a little show you may have heard of called *Watch Me Dance* where he plays a judge in a fictional dance competition. Now, Mr. Potts, it's your turn to play a *real* judge. How much fun are you going to have tonight?" She glows with giddiness.

"So much fun, Ms. Devereux!" he yells from the judges' table at the bottom of the stage.

"What's that?" She steals a quick look from me, and I nod my head up and down in the affirmative. "That's right you are. And capping off our judging crew is Xfinity Royalay. What a unique name for a unique woman of many talents. Ms. Royalay won the Arizona Senior Dancing with the Pros Competition at the state level last year and has returned to channel her expertise into the judges' panel. Please wave at your fans, Xfinity." A tiny woman, not much taller than the folding chair she sits on, stands up and waves at the crowd. She wears a simple black shift dress. Before sitting down, she pivots a full circle, shaking her hips before ending in a pose where she throws her arms up in the air as if to say *ta-da,* sending the crowd into a frenzy of applause.

"Now, my friends. Sit back into your comfortable chairs—unless you're sitting in the back row—should have arrived sooner! Ha! Ha! And be prepared to be wowed by our fantastically gifted professional dancers and our equally hard-working, talented locals. And thank you for supporting our local homeless shelter with your ticket purchase. Let the show begin!" she yells again into the microphone before stepping offstage next to me.

The music for the opening number begins with a low, quick bass. Two by two the local dancers and their partners come onto the stage, a rainbow of couples in their matching shirts. They spin and dip and cha-cha-cha in unison. I see Foster Stingerman sitting in the first row in an aisle seat. Lois told me before the show that he likes to get up and wander. Then Lois walks onto the stage in her sparkly silver shirt. No one would have been able to tell that the shirt had been fit for Waylon Tolly because Ingrid's fabulous tailoring makes for a perfect fit. Foster sits up tall in his seat, his eyes glued on his wife. He begins to immediately clap which makes everyone in the audience so uncomfortable with his solo clapping that they join in, too, filling the auditorium with thunderous applause for Lois. She takes a couple of awkward spins before Victor joins her and expertly guides her with a gentle arm around the waist with what can loosely be described as dance moves. But it fools Foster who thinks that his wife is dancing in the competition, and that's all that matters. What love she has for her husband to step out of her comfort zone to give him this joy.

"Remember, Safia. Lower your voice a little. The microphone amplifies everything that you say," I speak clearly into Safia's good ear, as she tells me that left is much better than right. She walks back to the microphone stand.

"Thank you. Let's give our dancers another round of applause for their opening act! Now, onto the competition. Each of our couples will dance twice. The first dance has been choreographed by our own Gerty Wilems." Gerty stands again and waves at the crowd. The judges will be looking for…"

My mind wanders away from the scoring criteria as I watch Lois tap Foster on the arm. She wears a medal around her neck that she shows him. He smiles from ear to ear. She takes his hand and leads him out of the auditorium. Tracy's old gymnastics' medal, worn proudly by Lois, now marks her "win" in the Southwest Arizona Senior Dancing with the Pros Competition, at least as far as Foster is concerned. It's nice when a ruse can bring so much joy.

Bob and Officer Lona are walking off the stage in their matching blue shirts when I turn my attention back to the stage. By the sound of the applause, they've done quite well. Amos and Ingrid follow with a series of moves from well-known dances, a bounce from a samba, a step, slide, step from a waltz, and quick hip shakes from a cha-cha. Amos is as smooth on the dance floor as he is with the ladies though I can't focus on anything but what Brenda had to tell me about Amos Aleger. Amos Aleger with the green truck—the same truck that had nearly run me over on the day of auditions? But why?

While Leo and Emma are dancing in crisp white costumes with a much less graceful dance technique, I message Officer Daniel about Amos's truck. I'd hoped to sneak offstage to tell him in person, but I don't see him anywhere. Caliope sits with Gabby in the fourth row. I love that my friends support the activities at Tucson Valley Retirement Community. A dancing competition is fun at any age.

I slide my phone into my back pocket as George and Tiffany, in black, slink onto the stage. I mean *slink*, too, because they've added matching detective hats, à la Sherlock Holmes style as they walk mysteriously to their places. There aren't supposed to be any deviations from Gerty's choreography, or points will be deducted, but as George is not going to win this competition, I applaud

Tiffany for encouraging a more fun presentation. Plus, the crowd will love their playfulness. They certainly aren't going to love George's dancing. Tiffany holds a large magnifying glass in her hand as she looks George up and down as if he were hiding something—perhaps an actual ability to dance? George plays along, shrugging his shoulders to the beat of the music. This dance might not score any points at all, but it's due for high laughs with the audience. I can see Brenda standing in the opposite wing of the stage where the female local dancers are awaiting their turns. She has a large enough smile that I can see it clearly from my vantage point. I look over my shoulder to see Amos who is glaring, not at George's performance on the stage, but at Brenda's enjoyment of George's performance on the stage. I feel a strong desire to protect Brenda from Amos more than my own self. I check my phone. Why isn't Dan responding?

"Wonderful! Just wonderful!" Safia claps into the microphone as the audience sits down after their standing ovation for George and Tiffany. "Oh, poodles! Look at the time." Safia mimics looking at a watch she is not wearing. "Do you know what time it is?" No response. "I said, *do you know what time it is?*"

"What time is it?" the audience asks in unison.

"It's time for the *ladies!* Let's give a warm welcome for our first female contestant, Renee Laruee, and her partner Vincent!"

"Woo-hoo! Go, Mom!" I watch Dad clapping with pride from his seat next to Keaton.

Harley Lawrence, cleared by Officer Daniel with a firm alibi on the night of Allen's stabbing, sits behind my dad. He's almost as enthusiastic for my mom as my dad. Odd.

Mom kills it. Her tap-dancing experience has clearly paid off. She pulls off the smoothness of the waltz, the bounce of the samba, and the quick moves of the cha-cha with ease. And more than that, she does it with a positive glow the whole time. I could not be prouder of her. Tracy jumps up and down from the other side of the stage as Mom and Vincent take their bows. I'm so appreciative of their friendship. There is much to be gained from having older, wiser friends.

"And now, Stu and Brenda," Safia says, giving the most lackluster introduction of a couple for the night. I have to give credit to a woman who wears her true feelings on her gold-sequined sleeves.

Neither Brenda nor Stu smile during their dance. The technique seems solid, but the whole performance looks stiff, even though Brenda is pretty in pink. I get the feeling that Stu wants to put this whole week behind him with the change in partners from Safia to Brenda. Was it an upgrade? The jury is out on that question. And Brenda wants Amos out of her life. I want him out of her life too. And out of Tucson Valley. What on earth does the guy have against *me?* It's sad that only one of our local female dancers—either Mom or Celia—will miss the chance to dance at the state level as they are both lovely dancers, but Brenda still deserves a spot due to the untimely death/not death of her partner.

Celia and Carlos, in red sequins, walk onto stage in the standard issue black pants like all the other dancers wear this evening though any comparison to the other dancers stops at the pants because Celia and Carlos have je ne sais quoi, that special *it factor* that Tracy educated us about on the day of auditions. When you know, you know. And watching the graceful fluidity with which Celia and Carlos move together across the stage, we *know*—everyone knows. Celia deserves that spot. Mario claps and yells wildly as she walks to her mark on the side of the stage to await the second dance.

"Wow," Bob says out loud. "That lady has the moves."

"Uh-huh."

"Yeah."

"Totally."

I look around me at the local male dancers and their partners who are offering their encouraging comments about Celia. She's not the lazy grump my mom's friends had pegged her for months ago. I smile at Ingrid who smiles back. Only Amos is missing. I look across the stage to see that Brenda is also missing from the wings where the female locals are gathered. Where is Officer Daniel? I want to step away and look for Brenda and Amos, but Safia is currently standing frozen on the stage staring wide-eyed in my direction. I look at the notecards in my hands and realize that she had given me her cards while Celia and Carlos danced while she took a bathroom break. I wave them in the air.

"Excuse me, please." She walks quickly across the stage, hiking up her skirt so she doesn't trip. After retrieving the cards from me, she uses them to dramatically fan herself on her way back to the microphone. "Sorry about that," she giggles. "It's getting *so warm* in here with all of these *hot* dancers, isn't it?" The audience laughs with her, eating up her exaggeration. "And now, on to the second dance of the competition, a freestyle chose by each couple to showcase their talents."

Mom and Vincent take center stage. The music begins, a rendition of Taylor Swift's "Shake it Off." Vincent takes Mom's hand and pulls her close before unfurling her while holding her at arm's length. The crowd erupts with applause even though Mom stumbles and Vincent has to catch her before she hits the floor. He reacts so quickly that it almost looks planned. A wave of pride washes over me, giving me a comforting sense of calm as she walks off the stage at the end of her dance. It's a really cool feeling to be a fully formed adult and to see your parent as a fully formed adult too—flaws and all—and love them even more.

"Brenda and Stu," Safia says dryly. *"Brenda and Stu,"* she repeats.

Stu steps forward until he stands next to me but no Brenda. Safia looks at me. I look at Stu. He shrugs his shoulders. It's at this moment that the lights go out, casting the auditorium and stage into complete darkness save for the safety lights on the emergency exits and on the aisle floors. "Excuse me. Excuse me." I push through the group of male dancers and their partners until I get to the hallway which leads to the fuse box. I bump into Mario who has the same idea.

"This is weird," he says. "The last time the lights went out, Allen was stab…Rosi? Rosi?"

I am pulled into Tracy's office and the door shut quietly behind me before I have a chance to say a word. And when I try to speak, a hand claps over my mouth followed by a bandana of some sort that is tied across my face.

"Let me be clear. You, Rosi Laruee, are responsible for the death of Brenda Riker and the injuries of that stupid man, too, though, I suppose you actually saved his life by being present when I pulled out the knife that was meant for you."

"Whhh…" I have so many questions I cannot ask.

"Why?" Amos laughs. "I'll be quick because your handyman will be fumbling for a key when he realizes you aren't still next to him. I am here for good, old-fashioned revenge. Your actions in Phoenix at the Senior Living

Retirement Community Conference led to the arrest of my sister."

"Sis…?"

"That's right. My sister is Adeline De LaVega. And you and your bumbling idiots that include that wretched woman Brenda deduced her plan to incriminate *you* in the death of Porter Price. All she wanted was to keep the Tucson Valley Retirement Community from getting that new tech canter. And if it hadn't been for you…"

"Medtheling kiddddddssth…" I fill in through the bandana.

"Right. She would not have gone to jail for the rest of her life. And Winding Creek Retirement Community would have built that superb technology center. You may not be going to jail, but where you are going will give her and I much joy, somewhere where you will never get in the way of a well-laid out plan again."

He taps something metallic against Tracy's desk. Another knife? I reach for Tracy's desk and feel my way around to the other side, grasping for anything I can find, a stapler, a pen holder, a potted plant, and start hurling them in the direction that I think Amos is coming from. I trip over Barley's dog bed that sticks out from under her desk and go sprawling to the ground just as something whizzes above me—the knife.

"Cripes, woman! Stand still! I promised my sister that I would—"

At that moment I hear the doorknob outside Tracy's office jiggling. "Rosi? Tracy?"

"You won't get away with what you've done to my sister!"

I push over Tracy's desk chair, sending it crashing to the ground.

"Stupid woman."

I hear something hit the chair, the knife's second attempt at bodily entry diverted.

Broken glass fills the room as Amos smashes something against the window. As the door bursts open, light from a flashlight fills the room. Officer Lona reaches for the bandana around my mouth. "Rosi! Are you hurt?"

I shake my head no, thankful for her arrival followed by Mario. "He's getting away!" I yell the minute I can speak again as I point to the window.

"Don't worry. Officer Daniel will take care of Amos. He's not going anywhere."

"Dan? He's here?"

"On the ground!" I hear yelling outside the window. "Amos De LaVega, you are under arrest for the attempted murder of Allen Elrod and the kidnapping of Rosi Laruee. Let's take a walk to my police car."

"But…I've been trying to talk to Officer Daniel all day. How did he know to be outside Tracy's office?"

Officer Lona clenches her teeth. "Sorry, Rosi. Officer Daniel asked me to put a tracer in your shoe. I was to keep an eye on things inside, and he's been monitoring things from his police car while talking to the crime lab in Phoenix."

"About what?"

"The prints on the knife. I got prints from Amos this afternoon from a water bottle after George messaged Officer Daniel about the green truck. He put the prints in the system, and they matched with an Amos De LaVega. He's a petty thief. And Adeline De LaVega's brother. That's when you got the shoe tracer. We had your back, Rosi."

I slip off my shoes. Sure enough, under the insert of my right shoe is a tiny tracer.

"I didn't feel it at all."

"I'm very good at my job."

"But I messaged Officer Daniel about the green truck. Why did you say George told him?"

"Because George *did* contact him—first. He'd been spying on Brenda and Amos. He told us he was worried for Brenda's safety."

"Why didn't you arrest Amos after you got the match on the fingerprints?"

"Officer Daniel knew how important this event was to you and to Tucson Valley. We really thought that Amos would behave until after the competition when he could be arrested quietly without causing an unnecessary scene. I guess Amos got antsy."

"Sorry about that," Officer Daniel walks into the room the minute the lights turn back on. "But I had everything under control, Rosi. You're not hurt, are you?" He puffs out his tiny chest with pride, assured of his plan to serve and protect.

"I'm not hurt. But Tracy's office might need a renovation." I look at the loose papers and office supplies strewn about the room.

"You always say that I need a better organization system. Oh, Rosi!" Tracy scoops me in her arms until Keaton enters the room, equally worried.

"Rosi? Oh, thank goodness. Rosi, are you okay?" He takes me from Tracy's grasp into his own tight hug.

"She's fine, Keaton. I had her protected the whole time," says Officer Daniel.

"It doesn't look like it," he says as he eyes the mess around the room.

"Sorry to break up this party…Oh, poodles! What happened here?" yells Safia.

"It's a…it's a story."

"I love a good story, but the dancers are waiting to finish the competition. Is that still going to happen? Mario has been holding everyone in the auditorium, since he took care of the lights."

"Yes, yes. We will finish this competition. No one tell my mother *anything* until this contest is finished."

"Rosi, are you sure you want to continue?" asks Tracy who puts an arm around my shoulders.

"I'm sure. We will finish what we started."

Chapter 23

The mood is quite subdued at the afterparty Tracy and I have organized to be held at the Spiky Cactus Restaurant. Dancers mingle with each other sharing conversations so quietly that it's hard to pick up the actual sentences unless you're in on the conversations. I'd wanted to cancel the party after Amos's arrest, but Tracy and Mom had encouraged me to reconsider, reminding me that everyone could use a nice distraction. *And a stiff drink,* Dad had said.

Celia proudly holds her trophy, a large statue of a male and female dancer holding hands in a dancing pose with a disco ball above them. She'd been the obvious choice. Brenda will be going to Phoenix for the state level of the competition though we'd only had one trophy. Surprisingly, she did not throw a fit when she was called onstage and received only a handshake from Safia rather than a trophy.

After Amos was arrested, I remembered that Brenda had also disappeared from the stage along with Amos, and I began to panic that she could be in trouble. As Officer Lona and I began to look for her, the door to the security closet opened, and out walked George and Brenda.

Let's just say that Brenda's pink sparkly top had become even looser, and her always perfect hair looked askew. And George had the biggest smile on his face that I've ever seen. George had been keeping tabs on Amos, and when he saw him step away backstage, he whisked Brenda to safety to protect her. True love at its finest.

I look out over the crowd of people that were mere strangers a week ago, now bonded together not only because of the Dancing with the Pros Competition but also because some maniac decided it would be the perfect event to enact his revenge and take me out. Just when I think that Officer Daniel will never earn his worth as a police officer, he surprises me. It's nice to feel protected. My eyes wander over to Keaton who is talking to Ingrid and Emma, and I'm not jealous one bit. I know. I know that Keaton loves me. I know that the past is the past, and we all have one. Without our pasts, we wouldn't have this chance at the present, and I wouldn't change anything if it had to happen this way to bring me to this moment in time—though a little less heartache in the breakup of my marriage might have ben nice. I also know that Keaton is *not* Wesley, and that Ingrid is *not* Cara.

Bob shares a laugh with Leo and Karen as he holds his trophy in one hand and a beer in the other. Amos would likely have won had he not been arrested. It's ironic that the one person who participated in the dancing competition with no real desire to dance had actually been the most talented.

"How are you doing, Rosi?" Dad locks his arm through mine.

"I'm okay, Dad. Thanks for being so supportive."

"Anything for my little girl." He kisses me on the cheek before joining Mom and her conversation with Jan and her husband Frank.

"Excuse me, Rosi?" A timid, though familiar voice, rings out from behind.

I turn around. "Hi, Brenda." George stands protectively with his arm around her waist.

"I wanted to thank you."

"Oh. For what?"

"You listened to me tonight. You…you cared. I knew it when you squeezed my hand. And Officer Lona told me how concerned you were for me. I don't get…I don't get a lot of concern in my direction, and…and I…thank you." She hugs me stiffly, and it's one of the nicest hugs I've ever received. "I also owe you an apology." Her eyes gloss over as George pulls her closer. "I'm sorry for being less than pleasant at times."

"Uh-huh."

"George and I had a daughter once, a little girl we named Rosa."

"I had no idea."

"We don't talk about her very often. She died when she was three. She would have been your age now."

I can hear my heartbeat pounding through my chest.

"I've been taking my grief out on you, and I'm sorry."

Things become clear in my mind as I begin to understand why Brenda has been so harsh with me. "I forgive you, Brenda. I'm so sorry for your loss."

"It was a long time ago," says George. "Our son is visiting us next month. He has a daughter he named Rosa, too. We'd like you to meet them."

"I'd like that. Thank you."

Brenda's eyes grow large as she looks past me. "Rosi, don't look now, but there is a handsome young man staring at you by the door. Be careful. Looks can be deceiving."

I turn around slowly. I've never been so surprised and happy at the same time as I am at this moment. I run across the room, bumping elbows into dancers as I go. "Zak!" I fling my arms around my only son, my baby who's a full, grown-up man.

"Hi, Mom. Surprise!"

By this time, my commotion has gained the attention of everyone in the room.

"Zak!"

"Hi, Grandma. Hi, Grandpa." They embrace him before pulling away to assess their first grandchild.

How could someone change so much in nine months? Zak has grown at least a couple of inches more, standing almost at 6 foot three, taller than Wesley. His brown hair has been neatly trimmed giving full attention not to his once curly locks around his ears but to his deep dimples on each side of his face. I can still see my toddler in the eyes of my grown son.

"I was able to change my flight from Chicago when my test in advanced calc got moved up. I thought a few extra days in the warm sun of Arizona might be nice. I hope it's okay that I'm early."

"Okay? Grandson, you've made these two women happier than a pigeon with a french fry." My dad pats Zak on the back.

"Where's your new friend?" I ask quietly, out of earshot of Zak's prying grandmother.

"She'll be here on Wednesday. You get me all to yourself for a few days." He gives me another hug.

I think my heart can't get any fuller than it is right now, but I am wrong. Keaton stands off to the side, by himself, not wanting to interrupt our reunion. I beckon him with my finger. "I'd like to introduce you to a special friend of mine." I smile at Keaton who smiles back with a hint of nervousness that I've never seen before. It's sweet. "Zak, this is Keaton."

Zak sticks his hand out to greet Keaton. "It's nice to finally meet you in person, Keaton. I've heard a lot about you."

He laughs. "Only half of it is true."

Zak laughs too. "Oh, I know. Mom likes to exaggerate when she's really excited."

And so, the teasing of the common link has begun. Now, my heart is full.

Just then the door swings open as another new guest arrives to the party. "Hello, everyone! I'm a…l…i…v…e…*alive!*" Allen yells with a huge smile on his face and a saunter in his hips as he kisses his Aunt Jan.

"What's that all about?" Zak asks.

I link my arm through his. "We have a lot of catching up to do. *A lot.*"

The Tucson Valley Retirement Community Cozy Mystery Series:

Book 6, Dying to Dink (Your Fault) will be out in April 2024.

Dying to Go (Nothing to Gush About)

Thirty-nine-year-old Rosi Laruee—named Rosisophia Doroche after her mother's beloved Golden Girls—decides that the end of her twenty-year marriage and her dad's impending knee replacement surgery are all the excuses she needs to visit Tucson Valley Retirement Community. But the drama follows Rosi when she finds the body of local tart and business owner, Salem Mansfield. The information she discovers using her newspaper reporter sleuthing skills coupled with the clues she picks up from lackluster Police Officer Dan Daniel lead to a surprise discovery when the murderer is revealed. Along the way, she meets a cast of characters in her parents' social circle who leave her questioning her parents' choices in friends while simultaneously befriending many of the residents, including a handsome landscaper and a brand-new Golden Retriever puppy she names Barley. Rosi's visit to Tucson Valley proves more than she'd bargained for, but maybe, she realizes, it's just the kind of change she needs. Laugh out loud with Rosi, and be prepared to get the happy feels along the way!

Dying For Wine (Seeing Red)

There's a rockin' concert of 1960s impersonators coming to Tucson Valley to perform in the snowbird send-off concert at the Tucson Valley Retirement Community Performing Arts Center. And as the one in charge, Rosi Laruee is thriving in the chaos. Diva attitudes, outrageous requests, and late flights don't sideline what is meant to be the greatest concert this community has ever seen. That is, until a dead body shows up below the stage next to the front row of seats. Now, she's sleuthing again with Officer Dan Daniel. Only this time, the murder is personal, and she needs to restore the reputation of Tucson Valley as being a safe place by solving this mystery quickly. What she discovers is a much deeper web of connections than she could have imagined. Throw in a condo search, a budding relationship with Keaton, and a growing Golden Retriever to Rosi's crazy adventures, and you have a recipe for hours of laughter.

Dying For Dirt (All Soaped Up)

It's conference time, and Rosi and her co-workers are headed to the Senior Living Retirement Community Conference in Phoenix. But don't think that it's time off! Joined by some of the most delightful and most annoying representatives of Tucson Valley Retirement Community, the trip almost ends before it begins along Interstate 10. Things don't get easier when, at the opening ceremonies, Rosi makes a most unfortunate introduction of herself. When her golden retriever puppy discovers a dead body that same night, Rosi pivots to sleuthing again as hilarity follows her every move.

Dying to Build (Nailed It)

Tucson Valley is weeks away from unveiling the new Roland Price Technology Center which will make them the envy of all retirement communities in the country. But just as things are coming together, a key crew member is found dead at the construction site, throwing an unwanted spotlight on the trials and tribulations that seem to follow Rosi Laruee as she discovers another dead body yet again. Up against the clock and the pocketbook, will the murder be solved in time for the scheduled opening ceremony?

Dying to Dance (Cha-Cha-Ahhh)

Things are booming at the Tucson Valley Retirement Community, and Rosi and her team at the senior center are very excited to be chosen as the location for the Southwest Arizona Senior Dancing with the Pros Competition where one female and one male resident will be chosen to compete at the state level. But things are never simple. When the professional dancers arrive in Tucson Valley to meet their senior partners, nerves get rattled and jealousy rages, leading to a most unfortunate ending for one unlucky dancer that may derail the improved status of the retirement community. Rosi is once again forced into an investigative role to make things right. Buoyed by the support of her boyfriend Keaton and the never-boring antics of her golden retriever Barley, Rosi just might be able to save the day before the drama dances away.

The Secret of Blue Lake (1)

The only true certainty in life is dying, but there's a whole lot of life to live from beginning to end if you're lucky. When Chicago news reporter Meg Popkin's dad makes a surprise move to a tiny town called Blue Lake, Michigan, in the middle of nowhere and away from his family after losing his wife to cancer, she wonders if there is more to the move than *just a change of scenery*. With the help of a new, self-confident reporter at the station, Brian Welter, she tries to figure out what the secret attraction to Blue Lake is for its many new residents and along the way discovers that maybe she's been missing out on some of the joys of living herself.

Drama, mystery, and romance abound for Meg as she learns about love, loss, and herself.

The Secret of Silver Beach (2)

After solving the mystery of the secret of Blue Lake, Meg returns to Chicago and to her new job as co-host on Chicago Midday. But when poor chemistry with Trenton Dealy leads to problems on the show, Meg is assigned a travel segment that will send her on location all around Lake Michigan visiting beach towns and local tourist attractions. The trip takes her away from fiancé Brian who has to continue anchoring the nightly news in Chicago. When odd threats start hurtling in Meg's direction, she finally confesses to Brian and those closest to her that she might have a stalker. Do the threats have something to do with the new information she learned about her dad's past in the little town of St. Joseph, Michigan, or is there something bigger at play that threatens more than Meg's livelihood?

Young Adult Historical Fiction:

War and Me

Amazon Reviewer: *The story and characters draw you in. I felt like I was in the story and feeling the emotions of each character. I laughed. I cried. I couldn't put the book down! The story takes place during the WW2 era and intertwines love with the realities of war. A must read!*

Flying model airplanes isn't cool, not for fifteen-year-old girls in the 1940's. No one understands Julianna's love of flying model airplanes but her dad. When he leaves to fly bomber planes in Europe forcing Julianna to deal with her mother's growing depression alone, she feels abandoned until she meets Ben, the new boy in town. But when he signs up for the war, too, she has to consider whether letting her first love drift away would be far easier than waiting for the next casualties.

War and Me

1943

Chapter 1

It's funny the things you do when you're paired against an adversary called *War*. The thought of collecting other people's junk a few years ago would have disgusted me. But if hunting for scrap metal to turn into weapons to defeat America's enemies would bring Dad home sooner, then I'd do it.

"Julianna, let's get down to the river," said Caroline. "Hurry! No way that boy's getting dibs on the scrap metal out there."

I couldn't stop staring at the unfamiliar boy across the river. He wasn't from Bridgmont. I was sure.

"Maybe we should walk down river a bit. I don't want to look like we're taking over his territory," I said.

"No way. We go upriver. Anything washing downriver he'll have first chance at. We're winning this contest. I need that money for a real dinner," said Caroline. "One night without rations."

We grabbed our boxes and headed upriver. I turned around and watched the lean, lanky boy looking at us. It was real quick, just saw his eyes darting our direction. I couldn't get a good look at his face, but something told me he was none too happy with our decision.

Caroline and I staked out a clear spot along the river. I rolled up my jeans to wade in the water. It was the only pair I owned, and it hadn't been an easy battle to win. I was never a prissy girl wearing bows in my hair or rouge on my cheeks, but convincing Mother had taken work.

"Let's look for long sticks," I said. When I turned around Caroline was already gone, traipsing through the woods like the tomboy she was, indifferent to the snapped twigs and broken logs in her way. She came back with two sticks before I even climbed over my first obstacle.

"Here. This will be perfect." She thrust a stick in my hand. "Just start poking around. Tomkin's is only a half mile up the road, and they put their trash out back. There's bound to be some tin cans washed down the river. I doubt those teenage boys he has working for him are as careful as he'd like. *You know how irresponsible we kids are!*" Caroline burst out laughing at her imitation of her mother.

Caroline often clashed with her mother. She always told Caroline what to do. *"Stand up straight. Make your bed. Wash the dishes. Clean those fingernails."* And she always ended by saying, *"Kids are just so irresponsible these days! When I was a girl..."*

At least her mother cared. She wasn't friendly, but she usually knew what Caroline was doing. My mother had no idea what my day looked like because she didn't ask. It was enough for her to just get out of bed. She didn't smile much. I tried to do everything I could to keep her content, if not happy. Nothing could make her happy with Dad gone.

Caroline and I worked for nearly a half hour finding twenty assorted soup, coffee, and vegetable tin cans. The mosquitoes feasted while we searched, and the humidity flattened my hair. Why I'd even bothered to use curlers this morning was beyond me. My hair always did best when left limp and straight. When I spotted an old bumper sticking out of the water halfway across the river I felt like my luck had finally turned.

"Caroline! Look!" I didn't wait for a reply. Stepping out on the large, jagged rocks that lined the shore of Hidden River, all I could think about was how we were sure to win the scrap metal competition at our high school if I could get that bumper out. Most kids would only bring in old cans or discarded tools.

As I stepped out on the third rock, I felt my confidence growing, and I began to imagine myself eating a big dinner down at Hannigan's Diner with my scrap metal earnings. While salivating with thoughts of buttered potatoes and juicy steak, I swatted at a swarm of gnats that were attracted to the water lilies growing on the water's surface. Before I could stop myself, I lost my footing on a slippery rock and landed in the cool river. I must have hit my head on a rock because the next thing I remember I was coming to in the arms of that strange boy from across the river.

Lanky Boy brushed my long hair out of my eyes and yelled at me.

"What are you doing?" I asked.

"Oh, good. You're awake."

"What are you doing?" I asked again as he carried me along the river's bank.

"I'm trying to make sure you're okay is what I'm doing." I reached up to touch my head, wincing at the throbbing pain. My hand was covered in blood. I felt like I was going to be sick.

"Julianna! Your head! We have to get you home," said Caroline, rushing over to my side. "What the hell are you doing?" She turned her attention to Lanky Boy.

"Seems that this is the question of the day. Just looking for a place to put your friend." He dripped water on my face, his hair plastered to his forehead. Staring at his brown eyes was the only thing that kept me from throwing up. Kinda like a milky chocolate bar, the kind Dad used to bring home sometimes after work before he left for war.

"Well, thanks for your help and all," said Caroline defensively, "But how could you have gotten here so quickly? You were downriver the last time we saw you. Are you following us?" She tossed her fiery colored hair behind her back and stuck out her chest. I guess Lanky Boy didn't like her tone because he deposited me on the ground, a bit too hard for my liking.

"Yeah, I guess you could say I was following you. Seems to me you're trying to steal all my tin cans, and that is not rightly fair. This is my territory, and I was here first."

"Well, let me tell you something, Mister!" Caroline fought back. "I don't see any name on this land, so it's free for all. You go to hell!"

"I think I need to go home now," I said. I didn't think a gash in my head would cause a battle in our sleepy little town, but now that it had, I just wanted peace.

"Hold this on your head until you get home," he said. "You'll be fine. The head bleeds a lot." He pulled off his shirt exposing his lean build. He paused only long enough for me to press the cool, wet shirt against my head. Lanky Boy was gone before I had a chance to thank him.

"Let's get you home. We'll take it slow," said Caroline.

I held Lanky Boy's shirt against my head which had stopped bleeding and leaned against Caroline's shoulder as we walked away from the river.

"I feel so foolish," I said.

"Hey, just think if you had managed to pull that bumper out. We'd be hard to beat for sure. That $15 first prize would definitely have our names on it. And how proud our dads would be to know that their daughters collected the most scrap metal."

"Have you ever seen him before?" I asked.

"Are you still thinking about that boy?"

"Just wondering if you've seen him around."

"No. He's not from around here. No local boy is going to ignore some fine beauties like us."

I laughed.

Caroline stopped, defensive.

"Why are you laughing? You laughing at me, Julianna Taylor?"

"You just make me laugh, Caroline. *In a good way.*" Caroline played by her own rules, but I admired her for that. And she was the only one I confided in about Dad.

"Dear heavens! What happened to you, Julianna?" asked Mrs. Hermann when we arrived at Caroline's home.

"I took a little tumble, Ma'am."

"And you're wet!"

"I got a little too close to the river."

"Caroline, get the peroxide."

Caroline did as she was told. Her mother was the only person who could ever make Caroline obey.

Mrs. Hermann examined my head. It still hurt, but there was no more bleeding. The peroxide was another story. I think being stung by a hive of bees would have hurt less that the sting of that peroxide on my head wound. I had to bite down on Lanky Boy's shirt just to keep from screaming.

"No stitches necessary. Why were you girls so close to the water? You need to be more responsible."

I could see Caroline rolling her eyes behind her mother.

"We were digging around for the scrap metal competition, Ma'am. I guess I wasn't too careful."

"Do be more sensible next time." She sighed. Did you collect anything good?"

"We collected a bunch of cans. I'm sure there's a lot more out there, too," said Caroline.

"You should go back and get your collection," said Mrs. Hermann.

"That would be nice, but you won't believe what happene…"

"NO!"

Caroline and her mother stared at me.

"I mean, no, there's really not that much there. It's not worth the trek back to the river. I'm sure someone else will find the cans anyway. I'd really like to go home now."

"Fine. I'll drive you home," said Mrs. Hermann.

"NO!"

"I mean, no thank you, Mrs. Hermann. We don't get too many warm fall days. I'd like to walk…with Caroline…if you don't mind."

"Be practical, dear. It might be diffic…"

"It's fine, Mama. I'll go with her. She's feeling better. I can tell, but she's right. She should get home."

"Then you best get going. Your mother will be wondering why you've been gone so long."

I really doubted that.

The scenery on my mile walk home complimented my mood. I really hated early fall. I knew winter was coming. Soon there'd be less daylight hours, and the snow would come. All the changes just reminded me more of Dad. I wondered what changes he was seeing. Where was he? Where did President Roosevelt send my dad? I'd heard that American troops had landed in Italy. Was Dad there?

"Thanks," I said when we arrived in my yard.

"For what?"

"For not telling your mother about the boy."

"It's fine, really. I don't need her hassles or nagging anyway. But what's the big deal?"

"I don't know. I just don't want her to tell my mother."

"About a boy that was obnoxiously rude? Why does it matter?"

"I don't really know. I just don't want her to know. I can't really explain it, Caroline." And I couldn't. I couldn't even explain it to myself. The memory of being picked up by the stranger with the brown eyes who'd come to rescue me wasn't something I could shake, and I didn't want to diminish it by talking about it.

"Should I come in?" asked Caroline.

"No sense. Mother's not in much of a mood for company. Thanks."

"Sure thing. And you might want to throw out that bloody shirt," she said gesturing to Lanky Boy's shirt which I still gripped. "It might concern your mother."

"You're probably right. See you soon."

I waved good-bye and tossed the stranger's shirt in the outdoor trash. I doubted Mother would even be awake to notice, but no sense taking any chances. She didn't need any more worries.

Mother was resting, as I'd assumed. It was her favorite past-time lately. I rinsed my long hair in the bathroom sink. I closed my eyes while the blood ran down the drain, wishing I could wash away all my worries as easily. When I finished, I examined myself in the mirror. My brown hair came from my dad, but my green eyes came from my mother, and sometimes, when I didn't have enough sleep, they had a hollow appearance, too. I always tried to get enough sleep. I opened the bathroom door. Mother stood at the top of the stairs, her hair stiff and ratty, pulling loose from her bun. The dark circles under her eyes told *her* story. It was my story, too. We shared the same story, but her pages were stained by tears. She couldn't see the happy ending I hoped for.

We both heard the mail fall.

Marcy Blesy is the author of over thirty books including the popular cozy mystery series: The Tucson Valley Retirement Community Cozy Mystery Series. Her adult romance mystery series includes The Secret of Blue Lake and The Secret of Silver Beach, both set in Michigan. Her children's books include the bestselling Be the Vet Series along with the following early chapter book series: Evie and the Volunteers, Niles and Bradford, Third Grade Outsider, and Hazel, the Clinic Cat. Her picture book, Am I Like My Daddy?, helps children who experienced the loss of a parent when they were young.

Marcy enjoys searching for treasures along the shores of Lake Michigan. She's still waiting for the day when she finds a piece of red beach glass. By day she teaches creative writing virtually to amazing students around the world.

Marcy is a believer in love and enjoys nothing more than making her readers feel a book more than simply reading it.

For updates, please click to subscribe to her newsletter.
https://preview.mailerlite.io/preview/745689/forms/108840024781358236
Follow updates on Instagram as well. @marcy_blesy

I would like to extend a heartfelt thanks to Betty for being the first person to read The Tucson Valley Retirement Community cozy mysteries and for giving me her guidance and expertise. Her personal pep talks are always welcome. She makes commas much less painful.

Thank you to the wonderful cozy mystery reader community who have been so kind and supportive of Rosi and her eccentric cast of characters in the Tucson Valley Retirement Community.

Thank you to Ed, Connor, and Luke for always championing my dreams and for believing in me. Thank you to Tom, Cheryl, and Megan for being such supports with my writing and in life.

And, finally, I'd like to think that my *Golden Girls* and *Murder She Wrote*-loving mom is smiling down on me, and perhaps, reading over my shoulder. Love you, Mom.

Made in the USA
Middletown, DE
30 July 2024